TEMPTATIONS

TEMPTATIONS

G. L. RAPULA

Published by Never Give Up productions and book dealers (Pty) Ltd.
388 Central House Building, Cnr Andries and, Pretorius St, Pretoria

nguproductions@outlook.com
www.nguproductions.coza

ISBN: 978-0-620-80482-0

Edited by Sifiso Sibanda
Cover design by G. L. Rapula & Khuthadzo Nephalama
Design and layout by G. L. Rapula

CONTENTS

"Both at the beginning of creation, and at the beginning of the recreation, temptation was the first event."

- **Pope Francis**

"A silly idea is current that good people do not know what temptation means. This is an obvious lie. Only those who try to resist temptation know how strong it is. A man who gives in to temptations simply does not know what it would have been like an hour later of being tempted. That is why bad people, in one sense, know very little about badness. They have lived a sheltered life by always giving in."

- **Clive Staples Lewis**

"The temptation to take the easy road is always there. It is as easy as staying in bed in the morning and sleeping in. But discipline is paramount to ultimate success and victory for any leader and any team."

- **Jocko Willink**

CHAPTER ONE

At six o'clock on Monday morning, she wakes up as the clock chimes. Swaddled in a woolly blanket against the cold, she starts preparing herself for the examination. She has a dream of becoming a qualified dentist, having her own family and being happily married. Of late family has become very important to her. She pursues her course at university because it provides her with knowledge. Besides, it teaches prudence and paves a bright future for her. The irony does not escape her mind: 'that the one who learns gains the keenest of lessons, while those who wait to be blessed remain nonentities'. It is an adage of her future profession, which she does not share with other people, because she doubts it will make sense to them.

Presently, she emerges from the bathroom cloaked in a robe, and goes straight to her twin sister's bedroom. Sitting on the bed, a bottle of whisky in her hand is Thandiwe, her twin sister. 'Don't you think you're running late?' she asks. 'It's already six o'clock and we're writing at ten. We're going to miss the bus!'

She pauses, waiting for Thandiwe to respond. 'I'm talking to you Thandiwe!' she shouts.

Thandiwe is silent and takes a sip. Then, 'I quit varsity,' she says finally.

'Has this anything to do with your sugar-daddy?' Thandeka asks in a voice filled with agony.

Thandiwe's eyes dart about in a squirrelly manner as she tries to avoid her sister's piercing stare but Thandeka is not willing to leave the room yet. Thandiwe does not really take kindly to judgement. Her first impulse is to react immediately. Why pretend to be a chum when in fact she does not have respect for anyone? Gently, decisively, she scrambles to her feet, and bends over to the other side of her bed. For a few seconds she searches for something. She picks up an axe from under the bed and flings it over her shoulder, over the bed towards Thandeka. A fling that should have undoubtedly killed her. However, it misses her and hits the wall. In a single quick movement, Thandeka dashes out of range. They are only twenty-two, not yet married, and are in their final year at the University of KwaZulu Natal, Howard College of Medicine, in the class of Health Sciences. Both have never known their parents. Their paternal grandmother, Catherine, raised them.

They live with her at No. 99 Farquhar Road Ladysmith, KwaZulu-Natal. Though Catherine earns no salary, she can pay for all the living costs every month in the house. She can pay the University fees for both of them. Thirty-five years ago, she moved from Richards Bay to Ladysmith with her husband, David Khumalo after they got married.

When David died ten years later, Catherine stayed in the cottage with her son, Themba. She had fallen in love with the place. She wanted to live a distance from home. She worked for "Sumitomo Rubber South Africa" in the nearby town of Steadville. The house is still a cottage, built with precast. However, it has been renovated and extended with four bedrooms, two bathrooms and has been roofed with concrete tiles, and walls have been painted yellow outside.It has become large, suitable for a big family. A vibracrete wall fence with a swing gate marks the front boundary. The rest of the front is lawn and a garden on the right. The way leading to the front door has been paved with paver walkway.

The floor inside is of a black tile, not expensive, but affordable. From the main door, there is a brown passage-leading straight through to the living room.

On the right, a blue doorway leads into the dining room and on the left is a kitchen, also painted blue. The rest of the rooms are cream-white. Next to the kitchen is a spare bedroom, then a living room.

Next to the living room is Catherine's bedroom, which has an ensuite. Between the dining room and the bathroom is a passage; a hallway that leads to Thandeka's bedroom on the left and Thandiwe's on the right. Outside the yard, next to the sidewalks, is a bus stop.

Staying with their grandmother moulded Thandiwe into promiscuity and alcoholism. As we meet her, she does not appear for the examinations, and never goes to the campus afterwards. She thinks she is beautiful. Thandiwe thinks her boyfriend finds her pleasurable. She can see him whenever she wants, and spend as much time as she pleases with him – at times she spends a full week in a hotel with him.

Outside her life, nothing matters. About her: clothes, men, cars, cash (she calls it) are trending; her main desires. About him, he does not want to say much of his life to her. He prefers to keep his life a secret – but gives her anything she wants. On Monday, the week after she quit university, she asked to meet him at the weekend, out of town. Then on Saturday, he makes it to her: he has booked one of the most expensive hotels in Durban, Blue Waters Hotel, out of town as she asked. Promptly, at four in the afternoon he checks in. The hotel itself: a glass table in the bedroom, a glass chair matching with the table, windows are also made of glass to match the theme.

Two white curtains conceal the windows. When the window is open, a soft breeze gently shuffles the two curtains. The sunlight streams across the floor, which is made of vanished wood; it still has the pleasant smell of polish.

When he enters, she is leaning on the windowsill, hands folded, waiting for him. She is wearing a pale summer dress, bare underneath, her hair is wet, and it seems she has been in a shower. As soon as he closes the door behind him, she is on him. She hops onto him: her legs hooked on his back, the velvet of her tongue inside his mouth. Gently, he lays her on the bed, takes off his clothes, and slides inside the sheets next to her. He makes love to her. Before she knows it, he is on his feet, gathering his clothes and leaving.

For a long time, she considers herself lucky to have him, even though they are not married, not even engaged. He is twenty-two years older than she is, but she is serious and committed to him, and even on that first night they spent together, she has always been thinking it would end up being a successful relationship. The following day she meets him at the same hotel room. In spite of his age, she somehow tries to find a quiet corner where she would ask him about his future with her.

'Do you have plans about us?' she asks.

A pause, cautious, trying not to give her an uncomprehending look. 'Us?' he mumbles. Actually, it is because he does not have any future with her, not in his realm, nor anywhere in the world in which he lives.

'Yes, us, baby.'

He does not take it as a question. Rather he tries to sentimentalize her, but avoids saying to her, 'I don't know. We have no life together.' She is too young for him; it might kill her.

'Let's not talk about that now, I don't want to ruin the surprise,' he says instead.

'Do you want to get married?'

'Yes… Of course,' he replies suddenly. She is asking sensitive questions, so stupid of her! Perhaps she loves surprises. However, it surprises her that of late he only enjoys her presence for a little while. He would like to spend an hour or two sometimes to strengthen her affection for him.

He has always promised her good things. However, things slip out of hands. Saturday afternoon in the city of Durban, she is alone; he is supposed to be at work as he arranged. Her eyes fall on him as she goes in through the entrance of the shopping centre. He is in Panarottis, sitting at a table with a woman and a child. She sees him kiss the woman. For a moment, she is not certain to conclude anything. The child has the man's lustrous hair and dark eyes. She can only be his daughter. However, it makes sense when he calls for attention to everyone and gives a speech, which Thandiwe barely hears. A few minutes afterwards, he sinks to his knee, and opens a ring box in front of her. It makes more sense when she allows him to slide the ring on her finger, and then they kiss. A few steps away from them, he notices Thandiwe, and drops his glance. She sets her eyes on the child; it literally resembles him.

She is pregnant, and it comes to her mind that he had affairs with many women. She ought to close her chapter with him, but it hurts mostly when she remembers how she has ruined her life for him. After this, she never saw him again; she spent all the time sobbing in her room.

CHAPTER TWO

Each day becomes eventless, featureless as a desert if she does not see him. There are days when she does not know what to do with herself when she does not see him. Sunday morning, Thandeka prepares breakfast before she goes to church. Thandiwe appears in Thandeka's room, wrapped in a blanket, hair unkempt, face swollen and entirely wearing a look of hurt. She is at a point of crying as she walks in.

'Is something bothering you?' Thandeka asks.

She shakes her head mutely. There is a long silence before she speaks. She looks into her eyes, 'He dumped me,' she finally says.

'Terry?'

'Yes,' she nods as tears begin to fill her eyes.

'I'm sorry.'

'I should have known I should have . . .' she says, and chokes on a sudden surge of tears.

Thandeka sits on the bed and draws her closer. They reach out for a hug and she begins sobbing miserably. 'You don't have to stress about that. God will...'

'Gosh! Stop it with your mental pollution; I have had enough about your God!' Thandiwe shouts suddenly.

Thandeka does not understand, but she keeps quiet. At the table in the kitchen, she appears. She is wearing a bathrobe and her feet are bare. She ought to eat but she has no appetite. She glumly stares out of the window: her expression has turned waxy and lifeless.

'Is there anything bothering you?' Catherine, the grandmother asks.

Stupid questions, she thinks. She does not reply.

'It's a sad story. She had a fight with… him… she just found out he is getting married…'

'Leave me alone Thandeka! You don't know anything about it.'

'Then you should eat and get some rest,' says Catherine.
She pauses, waiting for Thandiwe to respond. Now Catherine tries to take her in her arms. Gently, decisively, she wriggles free. She leaves them. Catherine trails after her to the bathroom, trying vainly to comfort her. However, Thandiwe bangs the bathroom door on her. They both know how she is when she is angry, so Catherine has to give up.

Within days, she has made up her mind about the child, she has no wish to have a child, and besides, it is too early to be a mother: 'No bitch ass fatherless babies in my system. Fuck it, fuck this!' she says to herself. 'Fuck this child and the bitch damn ass father!' she adds. She decides to abort the child.

CHAPTER THREE

On campus, Thandeka focuses more on her course. She spends more time in the university library, studying whatever she finds related to her course. While sitting at the library table, through the window, she notices one of the students she usually travels with on a bus every morning to the campus. The boy is on a path in front of the building in which she is. He is steadily gazing over her. His name is August Craig, a British final year student in the class of medicine. He enters the library and walks hesitantly towards her. She knows what is coming —women are sensitive to these things. She can tell from the weight of his desirous gaze.

'Hello,' he says.

She blushes. She rises from her chair to draw herself close but drops her glance. She is not a creature of romance. She wishes to walk away to avoid him. However, before she knows it, she has responded, offering an evasive and even a coquettish little smile like never before. He has all the physical traits that she likes. He has a milky skin, blue eyes, and thin pink oral lips. He is one of the quiet students in their medicine course – one that the female students on campus would hardly resist. However, for him it is not a big issue; the semester passes without him falling for one or other of his fellow students.They exchange names. He has no affair with any woman, not any of the dumpy, bustling immature young women with stupid behaviors. He does not like women who make no effort to be mature. He has resisted all young women in his life before. Nothing to be proud of, perhaps just a prejudice that has settled in his mind. Then, for the first time in his life, he likes someone. He likes, and desires Thandeka. She must be fortunate. They stand face to face, 'a beautiful young woman!' he thinks. Where has she been? His heart thumps with desire. She has thin lips, brown eyes, and long black hair. She tries to compose herself but cannot dismiss the truth that at the deepest level she is infatuated.

'I like your eyes,' he says.

She flashes another smile and says nothing in return. He stares at her, completely entranced. She lowers her chin to avoid his gaze. 'Do you mind if we try running into each other sometime, on purpose?' he asks afterwards. It is just a question. It does not come as a surprise to her. If she refuses, it is because of the way she sees things: the way she behaves to those men who follow her for copulation. In her high school days, she was dating one of the students in her class, but he was only after sex, which is something she did not like, something that compelled her to hate men.

'You are taking me out on a date,' she seems to be saying. Her words are clear. 'Of course,' she says. She wonders why she is so gentle with him.

The boy is not just any student. She has confidence in him — a string of joy for him. She has agreed to take a walk with him in the garden.

Unexpectedly, Thandiwe is on Campus. She is walking past the new crowded College buildings to the garden. The garden is a beautiful field of plants with rich manure: green shrubs with a pleasant smell of fresh fruit.

For a long time, she has not been on this campus and has forgotten how some of the things looked. She notices Thandeka with the boy. They are strolling in the garden, along the cloned wildflowers that bloom a thousand different colours. 'They can only be lovers,' she thinks.

'It's beautiful out here. I love walking among shrubs in this time of the year… it is … peaceful,' he says.

She is silent. Through her eyes, he notices that she shy to show herself in public. For the moment, Thandiwe is stalking them, hiding behind the trees, and following at a distance. A sudden surge of lust tugs at her. 'I have been there too!' she thinks. He thinks her beauty matches the flowers. However, he is not certain how to say it when he opens his mouth. He just met her a few minutes ago but something inside him gives an impression that he has known her for much longer. In the evening, he takes her to a restaurant near the lake. Thandiwe is still following. She has always been a girl of the city; she knows all its corners. She hides and waits patiently at a distance.

The windows overlook the lake and reflect the setting sun. In the main sitting area there are picnic mats laid on the floor for couples. There are wooden picnic benches on the opposite side. She chooses to sit at the table, at the corner. From where they sit, Thandiwe can see them clearly through the glass window. She gazes over Thandeka; she seems to be comfortable with him, she remembers herself growing up, thinking that she wanted to have this one day. Sitting across the table, they watch the sunset reflection on the lake. Lost in each other, they barely notice how fast time moves. They say very little when they eat, but are evidently pleased to be having dinner together. On their first date, he does not kiss her. Some girls are too sensitive. She might get a wrong idea of him. She prefers the kiss; it will make her night a very special one.

Perhaps, she enjoyed the night regardless of the excuse. Moreover, when she gets home, she asks her God if He could give her another chance with him. Thandiwe arrives a few minutes after Thandeka gets home. Thandeka is not aware the spying. Neither does Thandiwe mention the incident. Nevertheless, she has also liked him.

Indeed, she feels great tenderness for him. Thandeka has fallen in love, she must be careful.

CHAPTER FOUR

In the morning, there is a heavy downpour although it is winter. She walks to the bus stop under an umbrella. The bus comes immediately, but he is not on the bus. She walks up into the main entrance, crosses the parallelogram, and passes the school of engineering building to the Agriculture and Science Block. At the doorway, there is a small group of students waiting for a break in the downpour. He does not come though she waits for him throughout the whole morning.

She has a bad feeling. She is worried that she might have bored him. She is worried that she might never see him again. However, she is very wrong – he missed the bus because of rain. He misses all his morning classes and comes to campus in the afternoon. As for him, he believes in love letters. He regards them as romantic ideas. In addition, that they can last a lifetime because they tend to be special and meaningful.
It does not matter if he has no clue about how to write one. He just puts his fountain pen on paper and just lets his words flow. Before he could even know what he wrote, he would have expressed how he felt about the woman he loved.
The deluge continues throughout the day. Dark clouds from the west cover the city. At the end of the day, in her locker-room there is a letter from him.

Dearest Thandeka, with all the love in the world, I must apologise for not being able to see you today. I was stuck on the brink of the dangerous storm. I just want you to know, you are on my mind this morning. Moreover, I thought of you before I went to sleep last night, then in the middle of the night, you woke me up. Besides, I wish I could just telephone, to hear your voice, but I was scared to disturb your sweetest dreams. I know it sounds crazy, and I have no idea why I feel this way. I know I just met you, but I miss you. I believe you would not mind joining me for cooking tomorrow at my flat.
Yours,
August.

His words move her, they make her blush sweetly and go pink. A few minutes after she arrives at home he phones. Over the telephone, she agrees to join him for cooking. He offers to pick her from home. He plans an exotic menu for the following day. Before the sun sets, he is parking outside her house, about twenty-six feet ahead of the bustop, the spot she usually catches the bus every morning. He has known the place few weeks back when he has been studying her: he has seen her several times in the morning leaving her house late, having the bus wait for her.

He is not certain if she will come. However, when he lifts his eyes to the path towards the house; he notices her figure, walking to his car.

After a few minutes on the road with her —then, he holds the door open at his flat. Surprisingly, Thandiwe, the intruder who pays a detective agency to track the two down is aware of their arrangements. She follows. For now, she has his Name, and his address. She has to find his number. In the kitchen, he lets her chop onions, tomatoes and cilantro while he prepares a chopped deli-roasted chicken. What he throws for supper is very simple: Mexican Chicken salad. They eat outside on the patio, and then lie supine on a mat, on the floor with a picnic basket filled with late night snacks for desert. They watch a show of falling stars; she is staring in amazement as the lashes of white is racing from corner to corner of the sky. Spending time with him brings a question to her mind: she wonders if it was possible to resist the desire to be with him. Things become difficult when she does not see him. There is usually nothing inside her mind, except him. They spend most of their time at the university library, studying. Then spend the evening together.

They want more of each other, and no matter what happens between them, they already know that they will never forget anything about each other —but they never mention it, they never talk about it. Every night she sneaks home late because her grandmother does not know about her affair with him. However, for Catherine, falling in love could have fallen out of fashion on her side but she is fully aware of Thandeka's moves. Nonetheless, there is nothing wrong with falling in love; love eases the awkward moments in life for all she knows.

It would not be a contention to accept it.

'May I invite you to stay with me for the weekend?' he asks.

A pause, cautious. She is silent, dubious.

'Come on, it's going to be fun,' he pleads.

'Do you do this kind of thing often?' she asks.

'Do what?'

'Invite your girlfriends over.'

'I have no interest in girls.'

'Aren't you interested in me?' she asks.

'I am.'

'Why don't you tell me?'

He is silent. He tries to find something to say.

'Do you love me?' she says without thinking.

'Of course, I do.'

'Why don't you tell me?'

She doubts it.

However, if she gives up on him, she will remain useless; it is what she thinks. Her irony: those who do not engage with what they have interest in, will learn nothing about it, they will be useless to their desire.

On Thursday, she comes home early. Catherine is sitting on a sofa watching television. She sits with her for a few minutes. 'How are your classes?' asks Catherine.

'Just fine.'

'Are things working out?'

'Yeah.'

'Good. You will have to give it more time to make it work.'

A pause, waiting for Thandeka to say something. *Of course,* Catherine would expect her to say it in return. However, something different waves into her ears: 'Would you need me this weekend? In the garden?' she asks instead.

'No.'

'I will be with one of my colleagues, revising for a test on Monday.'

'I'm so proud of your hard work,' says Catherine.On Friday night he ushers her into his flat again. On a table, he serves her a simple roasted chicken and salads. In addition, throws chocolate fondue for desert. He studies her as she eats. She lacks nothing; she has the virtues of kindliness, maturation, he thinks. What a pretty girl I will be involved with, he thinks.

CHAPTER FIVE

After Thandiwe has finished investigating him, she has almost all his personal details. She has his full names, his address, his telephone number, and his lectures' slots. Even his parents' names. According to his timetable, he does not have lectures on Thursdays; he is usually at his flat. After getting his number, she waits for a few days, and telephones him on Wednesday at nine in the evening, when Catherine and Thandeka are already in bed. 'Hello?' she says.

The voice he hears belongs to someone he thinks is Thandeka, not a stranger.

'Hey. How are you?'

'I'm good, thanks,' she says. In her voice, there is a hint of excitement. 'May I please speak to August Craig?'

'Yes. I am.'

She waits, takes a deep breath. 'I'm Thandiwe. When can I see you?'

'I know who you are,' he says. Though she has introduced herself, he does not sense anything different from Thandeka. He does not even know the difference between the names Thandiwe and Thandeka. 'When do you want to see me?'

'Tomorrow. Perhaps you might like to go out for lunch,' she says.

'I'm okay with that.'

'Meet me at Malis Indian. Shall we say, at twelve?' Malis Indian is a restaurant in the city of Durban.

'No problem. See you at lunch.'

When she puts down the telephone, her face is puffy with a playful, quality smile. What a good move, she thinks. The following morning, she wakes up at eight and prepares. First, she goes to a hair-saloon and fixes the hair. Then goes to a shopping centre at ten. Her attire is the main bait to get the full attention of a man. She buys a white short-tight dress, and a Gucci, cotton-blend trench coat. What she is planning to do is not right; the man is a boyfriend to her sister. Who knows, there might be a future for them. There is still time for her to wriggle out. However, she is too excited, and the moment passes. She arrives late, thirty minutes late after their arranged time. When she arrives, he is the first person that she notices. He is sitting at a table for three, wearing a black suit, whose blazer neatly hangs behind his chair. She waits, fixes her coat before she catches up with him. 'Hello, handsome,' she says. There is a smile on her face.

The face he is looking at is not very strange. It took after Thandeka: eyes, lips, and thickness. The difference is their skin; Thandiwe is a bit lighter than Thandeka. 'Hey. Can I help with something?'

'I'm Thandiwe. And you must be August, right?'

He nods, offering a blank incomprehension. 'Yes.'

'I'm Thandeka's sister. We spoke over the phone last night.'

He raises his chin, examining her. Her Trench dress, he notices, exposes her thighs. 'Okay,' he says. 'I was expecting Thandeka. May I invite you for a sit?'

'Thanks. I told you my name. Moreover, there is a difference between Thandiwe and Thandeka. Thandeka is my sister, my name is Thandiwe.'

'Nice to meet you, Thandiwe.'

His expression wears a perfect tranquil. It however, does not dismiss the hint of puzzlement on it. She lets him order. Let the guest lead, and the host will follow, she says to herself. He orders two risottos, and a bottle of wine. They eat in silence. She waits; her eyes are set on him as he eats. He is not aware of them, but he eats carefully: nothing so distasteful to a stranger. 'So. Handsome,' she says, 'How can a white, handsome young-man like you, fall in love with a normal black young woman?'
He has stopped eating. Cautious. 'What do you mean?'
'I was just saying. You know, it is unusual for a white man to be involved with a black woman. You seem a bit different, charming, and kind.'
He smiles. 'I like people, despite their race. I love everyone.'
She is casting a steady gaze over him and she is wearing another smile.
He first clears his throat. 'What?' he asks.
'I am just wondering, what you would do if I told you how attractive you are.'
He is silent before he speaks. Then, a cautious, 'Thank you.'
'Are you looking to get a new partner?'
He is silent again. She ought to let it go, but she does not. Instead, across the table, she rises from her chair and strolls around him.
'I too like you, August,' She says with a romantic gentle voice. She stops behind him her hands gently rubbing his chest. She leans over him, her chin is drawn, rests against his cheek. 'Do you like me too?'
He glances over his watch, clears his throat again. 'Excuse me,' he whispers, 'I have business to attend to.' Gently, he wriggles loose, rises and picks up the blazer. 'Thanks for the lunch,' he repeats and leaves.

CHAPTER SIX

He has been on Thandeka's books for about a year. Thandiwe has also been trying to put him on her own books too, for over a year. However, he does not tell Thandeka about it. He does not even mention the incident at the restaurant. He prefers to keep it within his chest; he does not want to ruin the relationship of the siblings. Nevertheless, as much as he tries to keep it a secret, Thandiwe keeps coming to him. He gets used to it, but he must learn this: Thandiwe does not give up on her desire; she will never release her grip, not now or anytime soon.

He must always keep it in mind or else she will irritate him. Nonetheless, Thandeka has learnt many things about him. From what she knows of him, he is calm, open, and kind. He has talked a lot about himself with her, a lot about his life. He is a good boy, almost as good as she thought he was the first time; she is beginning to learn his sentiments. His sentiments are, he is uxorious, willing to sacrifice, faithful, considerate, and even decisive. It did not take too long for the two to learn about each another. They have mutual understanding, mutual goals about the future. Their story is quite amusing. Quite strange, strange enough to grip her attention. She is wondering how things have gone so fast.

During their first weeks, August and Thendeka found themselves falling in love without even noticing it. A year passes and they graduate together. A few months after graduations, life begins. From now on, they will live the life that they always wanted to live from their childhood. A life that they worked the years of their University days for. He spends the first six moths working at a government hospital, helping as much as he can. It has been part of his dreams. However, with a fortunate sequence, he receives assistance from department of health and opens his surgery at a private hospital, Busamed hillcrest hospital, while Thandeka works as a professional dentist at Lady Smith Hospital, the hospital in her hometown.

About Thandeka's affair with August, Catherine feels a growing joy as she transforms herself into another woman (the in-law-grand-mother, she calls it). She is widowed; and for this matter, she regards it as a wedding present. She emerges with a smile, which she offers Thandeka, then reaches down to pet her hair and kiss her on the cheek. Perchance something bad happens to Thandeka in her relationship with the boy; Catherine would be the one to rescue her, for she knows all. It would not be for the first time –Catherine has been and will always be on the scene for her.

He would like to spend his life in a relationship with her. She continues to love him because it provides her a good moment of life. It is an important feature of their relationship. Sunday morning, he drives her to church with her grandmother. At ten, the same morning Thandiwe is at his rented flat, she is hiding behind the bedroom door waiting for him. When he walks in, she has given him no warning: she jumps over him, kisses, snatching him. 'No, not now! Stop!' he says, struggling. She is too greedy for him; she is in no state to stop. In fact, nothing will stop her. She strokes his neck, throws him on the bed and brushes off his shoes. For now, he does not wish to resist anymore. Instead, the scene changes; he is the one who lays her out on the bed and undresses her. As soon as she is bare, he kisses her feet, and turns her back to him. A woman with a beautiful skin, a milky skin. He finds it pleasurable; no man would ever resist it.

'Please. You must go,' he says when it is over. 'Thandeka might be back any minute.'

She obeys: she rises, gathers her things, tries to kiss him but he does not allow her. When she has left, he sits with his hands on his face, unable to move. He is dejected. A mistake, a huge mistake. At this moment, he doubts it; he does not believe it has happened. This is not him, he says to himself. His heart, his spirit, his whole being at this moment is flooded, puffy with dullness.

The same afternoon, he has arranged to pick Thandeka at church but he does not come. At four o'clock, he telephones offering to pick her at Catherine's house. When he arrives, she is waiting on the sidewalks outside the house, opposite the bus stop. She is waiting with Thandiwe. They talk briefly and then laugh. He pulls before them; Thandiwe is wearing a pair of summer shorts that he finds silly. Comfortably, she comes to greet him with a smile. 'Take care of her,' she says to him afterwards and leave.

What a snake of a woman, he says to himself. During the drive, he fears to look at Thandeka. He is silent, listening to her speaking. She tells him about the church service, but he does not pay much attention. At the kitchen, she sits on a stool, watching while he cooks. Then he sets a table. They eat in the dining room, open a bottle of wine, and drink in a cup. She dishes up a second plate. A healthy appetite for a happy woman, a woman that I have betrayed, soon to be my wife, he thinks.

Though he has cooked, he has no appetite.

'Is something bothering you?' she asks.

He is silent. He remains, looking at his food. He is thinking about
   the incident. What kind of man, stupid man who cannot resist
   anything. A man who failed to resist a stupid woman.
Softly she speaks his name. 'August!'
He does not hear her. She clears her throat. 'August!' she says,
   loudly.
Everything that he has been thinking about is broken. 'What?'
'Is something the matter?'
'No. I am very well,' he says.
'It was so nice,' she says, drains her cup. Then rises, gathers her
   stuff. 'Thanks for the supper,' she adds and tries to leave.
'Don't go yet.' He takes her by hand. First, a pause –then:
   'Please spend the night with me.'
His face is strained, expresses displeasure; she is aware of the rise
   and fall of his chest. 'Why?'
'I just want your company.'
She can even sense the hint of breathlessness in his voice.
   Another pause before she speaks. 'Ok. But I have to be home
   before the sun rises.'
'Deal,' he concludes.
In the bedroom, on the bed-top, he has designed an emblem of a
   heart with roses. He turns on the lights and puts on a music in
   the stereo: The Manhattans quintet. He is standing, unable to
   move. Whatever that he would like to do is either he did not
   plan for it or he does not have an idea how to do it. As for the
   music, it hovers somewhere else, not in his ears. He can hear
   the instruments, but it does not win his attention, he does not
   even hear the melody. Nonetheless, what is it that he wants to
   do?
That is what he thinks about love and death with a passionate
   young woman. He takes her hand into his, and speaks.

However, the simple words that he ought to say are heavy as
feet stuck on a sea of mud. 'You know I am determined to be a
good lover to you. A good lover and a good person. But I end
up being a bad person because of my weaknesses.'

He puts his hand on her cheek. 'You know you mean a lot to
me,' the words are now coming fast, 'and you know I have so
much love for you.'

She is silent. Her eyes are defiantly set on him; her face wears a
curious gaze.

'I want to ask you for something,' he sinks to a knee and searches
for something from his pocket: a wooden ring box bearer
bearing a cushion cut natural diamond ring.

'For the gift you are to me, I would like to spend these last best
days of my life with you, as my deepest love, the very best of
me,' he says.

'Thandeka Khumalo, will you be my wife?'

She is silent. Yet at her moment of enthusiasm, she sucks a mucus
running from her nostril. Then chokes on a soft tingling joy of
tears. She nods in silence before she speaks. 'I will,' she says. 'I
would like to be your wife.'

She is smitten with the jewelry: jewelry prodigal of beauty, of
beauties. He folds the bedclothes aside, touches her wet cheeks,
kisses her, starts stroking her honey skin; he makes love to her.
It is for the first time the two make love to one another; it feels
good. However, what Thandiwe has given him was very good,
more joyful than this. It was not rape, he was not totally in a
mood for it, but he enjoyed it. Though Thandeka is not as good
as Thandiwe, he enjoys it with her too. She will soon be his
wife, so he ought to accept it.

CHAPTER SEVEN

The following day is Monday. A day that she, if anything, finds more beautiful. She wakes up before him. It is the first time for her to wake up with a man beside her in her life. She disappears into the kitchen and when she returns, he is awake. A flurry of happiness runs through him, strong enough to take him by surprise when she serves him breakfast on bed, before he goes to work. This is how their days will be: serve one another breakfast. When he looks at her, there is a big smile on her face. A pity that must be his theme, but he is in no state to say anything. He steals another glance at her; she is a perfect, a good young-woman. He does not say I laid your sister on this bed yesterday before I laid you. Nevertheless, he thinks fruit of the same tree probably have the most intimate detail. Yet there are differences: different pulsing of blood, different urgencies of passion, etcetera. He is a true believer when it comes to the idea that surprises and passion are the bedrock of any good working affair. He has something in mind —this is where it begins. The same morning, with a surprising precipitateness, he gives her an envelope; it bears the couple's tickets for seven days gateway by a Yacht to a sunset beach in Cape Town. His first instinct the whole week is to book a flight, then call a driver to pick them up at the airport. He spends the week afternoons in the surgery, working as far as he is able. When the last of the day's surgery is over, he helps her pack the bags. Then Friday, at eight in the morning, he unlocks the padlock on his remote control and lets it roll up the garage door. She has not heard the last of his surprises. He casts a glance around a brand-new car, a car that he has bought for her, for the woman that he will soon be calling his wife. A 2017 Mercedes-Benz C63 AMG Edition 507.

'Oh my God! It's nice.'

'Do you like it?'

'Of course, it's beautiful.'

'Take,' he passes the keys. 'It's yours.'

'What?'

'It's yours.'

There is silence.

'Take,' he repeats.

'It's more than just a car, August!'

'Don't you want it?'

'I do. But...'

'Take,' he still offers the keys. It takes a while before she accepts them.

To some degree, she is not a lover of surprises; she often doubts she will ever be. Surprises do not suite her, it is just an irony that she likes. However, she accepts it.

'Thank you,' she says afterwards.

He helps her toss the bags into the car boot. Two minutes later, she is driving on a main road, heading to Pietermaritzburg Airport (PZB, FAPM) in the city of Durban.

After a few hours from the airport, the two land at the Cape Town International Airport (CPT, FACT). Then appear in Gans Bay Harbour, Western Cape. The harbour is crowded, of men and women walking hand in hand. It looks like a valentines' day. Businesspersons rolling their luggage behind them occupy the boats. They wait behind; he has booked a prodigal Excellence III Yacht Charter for him and her, only. The floor of it is made of varnished African wood, made and built to last for a long time. In the bedrooms, the roof is made of glass. It offers its ocupants a full view of shooting stars. A balcony runs around the main bedroom. The top roof offers a refreshing foaming plunge bath, which is pleasant-smelling and dimly lit.

In the field of sex, her temperament is intense, and so is his passion. He has never been intrinsic about copulation. If he has been a lover of women from his childhood, before he met Thandeka, he would be, or has been, a professional of sex with every woman he has met.

Nightfalls, they sleep together merely as children do, cuddling, touching, giggling, re-living friendship more than lovers. At midnight in the bedroom, he suffers from insomnia. It haunts him; the image of Thandiwe keeps coming to him. 'Make love to me,' says she, her words are clear, urgent. Wherever the bitch is, she must be sleeping, comfortably enjoying whatever stupid vision she is having, he tells himself. He stays wide-awake late into the night, dealing with the dirty memories that come to haunt him. In the morning after sunrise he is dead asleep, covered in a sheet, drawn up to his eyes; she is awake, and presently disappears into the bathroom. Later he wakes up, the midday hour is approaching, and Thandeka is out of the bathroom. Roses are scattered on the floor on the path in the balcony. Following the roses, he appears at the balcony. A glare around, breakfast is set at the table. He notices her. She is dressed in his white oversize-shirt, naked beneath, standing at the balcony.

The shirt exposes her thighs. Though she is not thoroughly naked, he can see the brownie skin and vulnerable tendons of the backs of her thighs when the wind blows over her. She is carrying two wine glasses and a bottle of champagne. She approaches him, puts the bottle and glasses on the table, embraces and kisses him fondly. What a wonderful morning kiss! 'You want something to drink?' she asks.

'Yes, please.'

She opens the bottle and pours into the glasses; one is for him. He studies her, it is the first time he notices it: she has a young, pleasant, and more than just a pretty face. A year ago, she was just another pretty face on the bus, in class, on the campus. Now she is a presence in his life, a breathing presence.

'You have a pretty face. I love you,' he says.

A smile flashes. 'I love you too,' she responds.

She sips the Champagne and smooch it into his mouth, he embraces, and kisses her passionately. The moment passes. After a few hours, the boat approaches Robben Island. The sun has set – not more than an hour ago. The water is cosy – on the top roof, the two have planned a candlelight dinner. The warm glow of candles makes everything seem so smooth and misty; the soft candlelights make her skin colour sexier. A smooth colour that would tempt anyone to a sexual desire, mainly with her. He is less hungry than he thought he would be. Thandiwe still haunts him, but somehow he tries to finish the meal. No matter how hard he tries to hide it from Thandeka, the truth always has its own way of coming out. One day, it will find a way to her, let him be aware of it. Thandeka is a true believer, faithful to her God, and her God will find a way to expose those who are not true to her.

Enough! It irritates him; he has had enough of it. Decisively, he rises from his chair, lifts and carries her into the bathroom, draws a bath with candles surrounding the foam-bubble bath. He lets her slip in first, and then follows. He stretches out his

pale length in the foaming water and relaxes. They just soak in
the water, fool around for a while, and make love.

CHAPTER EIGHT

He has been in her hooks for over a year and months —he finds her entirely attractive. Because his affection for her is not falling, he believes it is mutual. He has introduced her to his family in Britain. No matter what passes between them now, falling in love, , may fall out of fashion, but it would come back again half a dozen times. Being together is good, as good as the first time, for all he knows. They migrate into their new house in Pietermaritzburg, after that they get married. The first time he has lived with a woman on his own. He lived his childhood only in the presence of his parents; he ought to control his manners. At least, try to be neat.

Thandiwe still takes refuge in her grandmother's house, in Ladysmith. As months pass by, Thandeka begns to think about Thandiwe's future for the first time in her life. For a woman of Catherine's age, fifty-nine, she earns no living, rather depends on the sale of vegetables in her garden.Thandeka tries to save as much as she can, to provide for her grandmother and her sister. However, before the third week of the month, Thandiwe spends all the money. Though she suspects that Catherine and Thandeka knows what is going on, Catherine never says anything directly to her. Not because she is afraid of her, but because it is not her business. Saturday evening, Thandeka comes to visit for the weekend. At a table, they eat supper together. They have been a family, a wonderful family.

'This is so nice,' says Thandeka. 'Do you always cook, Thandiwe?'

'Of course. I live with Catherine, and she is too old. If I don't cook, who else will?'

'I suggest you find a helper.'

'Why? I really don't hate it.'

Thandeka is silent.

'What will I pay her with, beside?' she adds. Her words smack of violence; they aim to cause a scene. Catherine silently wishes the scene would not come.

In fact, she is the one who ought to stop it. She begins to talk entertainingly, to distract Thandiwe. She talks about their childhood before their parents left, about Themba, the man whom they never met but they know him as their father. Though she talks about him, she does not mention anything about his disappearance.

'He is a good young man,' she says, turning her gaze on Thandeka, 'you took after him, his behavior.' There is a smile on Thandeka's face.

'What about me?' Thandiwe asks.

'People say you took after me. They say I used to behave like you when I was young.'

'Do you agree with them?'

'I don't know. I do not remember. I was young.'

Thandiwe has lost interest in the meal; she shows her interest in the conversation. 'Grandma, you haven't told us exactly why mom and dad left us,' she says.

A long pause from Catherine, then cautiously. She does not want to meet their eyes but replies with slow and heavy gestures. 'Your parents just left because they wanted to leave.'

She does not wish to continue this talk. She loses appetite too, whatever question will follow; she does not wish to answer it. She still has time to tell a lie, she wriggles out of this conversion.

'Left because they wanted to leave? You mean they just abandoned us, easily just like that?' asks Thandeka.

'Your parents would never abandon you.'

'If they have not abandoned us, why aren't they coming to visit us in the first place? We are twenty-five now, I am married but I do not know who my father is, and who my mother is. I do not even know if they are still alive or dead. Nor do you?'

'Enough!' she retorts. 'I said I don't know. I have no further question to answer.' She rises from her chair and disappears into the bedroom with shame and a heavy heart.

Thandeka and Thandiwe suspect something. However, they are not willing to bother her. It is possibly because they have given up on their parents. Even if they have a desire to know more about them, it has to stop here. Catherine is not the person to answer these questions. There is nothing to say about it. It ends here, and ends now.

CHAPTER NINE

Close to midday on Sunday. Catherine has gone to church; Thandiwe is alone in the house. She is hanging laundry behind the house. August, the one who, if anything, hates Thandiwe by all her nature, turns off the road on the track that leads him to work and appears at Catherine's house.

Thandiwe does not expect visits before midday on Sundays. In fact, she does not expect him to come anywhere near her. All animals know what to expect when a predator enters their nest. She would expect violence from him, a serious scene whose elemental rage she has never felt. He would like to give her what she deserves: a sound thrashing. A knock at the door. She goes to open wearing the same summer shorts and slippers that she finds entirely silly. 'August?' she says. 'I wasn't expecting you to be here. Catherine and Thandeka are not home.'

He gazes over her thighs, a smooth, attractive milky, blue-veined skin. 'May I come in?'

'Sure,' she replies, and dubiously ushers him in. She holds the door open for him and flattens herself making him some space to pass. 'Can I invite you for tea, juice or...'

'You so sexy in those outfits,' he says, standing on a path leading to the living room.

What a pretty girl with her own ways of wooing a man.

She tries to speak, but nothing comes out of her mouth. After a long pause, 'Oh, really?'

Does she know he might have an eye on her? Perchance, she knows of him, she discovered his weakness the time he made love to her. There are virtues of complete passion she sees in him, which she would wish to prolong forever. She drops her glance with a coquettish smile. With no warning, he is on her: he slides his velvet tongue into her mouth. His hands fumble under her shorts. There is no resistance from her, she takes him by hand to her bedroom and lowers herself on the bed. He peels off her scant clothing and starts making love to her; she hooks her legs behind him to draw him closer and puts more pressure on him.

When he has finished, she is lying beneath him, her eyes closed, her hands slack under her head, a coy smile on her face. He is perfect; she will need him more often.

When it is over, he frees himself, gathers his things to leave, but she still wants more of it. It felt good and joyful, but he ought to leave before Catherine finds him. There is only one way to avert her: for the session, he pays her R3000. He kisses her, kisses her breasts, and reaches to his car and drives off. This is Thandiwe. Anyone who does not know her knows anything.

She is not a fool. She does an enormous amount of good to people, specifically to Thandeka. She cares a lot about her, but then, for the bill that August pays her, she will find a way to him. Regardless of what comes, there is always going to be a space for her to fit. She often toys with the idea that she belongs to him. She receives R4500 every month from Thandeka, which she out to spend on food and clothes. However, she has also stacked the fact that for each session, August will pay her more than what she has been receiving from Thandeka.

Then, for August, what does it entail, being a husband? In his mind, he does not think about it. Though he is a husband to her own sister, a person that ought to matter the most in her life, she does not seem to care about it. All that matters is that she ought to embrace the role that the world had laid out for her; she has a duty to celebrate it. Every Sunday she prepares for him to come when Catherine goes to church. Sometimes they meet when

Thandeka works late from the hospital. When her shift is at night, before the midnight when Catherine goes to sleep, he comes to Thandiwe, and often comes when it rains.

CHAPTER TEN

Thandeka respects is her husband to solidify her marriage. She humbles herself before her husband. She does it not only to arouse him to love her, but to exhort him as well. She always wanted a fruitful man, a man who could love and respect her too. She often battles against her own feelings: no one can occupy his space in her. For many times she uses biblical commandments to justify her role as a wife. She is always in church every Sunday. On this particular Sunday, August is with her, sitting next to her in the pew. In a little while, the pastor appears in the altar. 'Hallelujah *Bazalwane!*' he shouts. 'Let's stand up and pray.' The congregation starts praying. During the service, he preaches on the book of Proverbs 31:10.

"Who can find a virtuous wife? For her worth is above rubies."

'Amen.' the congregation replies.

He continues preaching about being a Godly wife to a husband: 'Women should always remain unshaken towards their goal of building a strong companionship with their husbands,' he says. 'As long as you live, do well to your husband, and never harm him.

Desire good values in everything that you do: speak gently in wisdom, for that God will give you a credit for all things you do. Because a woman who honors the Lord should be praised...'

In a moment, August disappears during the church service. After a few minutes on the road, he arrives at Catherine's house. Thandiwe is alone, as usual. He first knocks, but the music is too loud in the living room. She cannot hear him, but she sees him through kitchen the window. First, she goes into the bedroom, and clears the bed, then takes off her clothes as she returns and open the door wearing one of her best lingerie, a pantie and a bra. She already knows what he wants. In fact, she has been waiting for it to come, waiting longer than he knows. Her body is almost perfectly clear, so he does not waste time: he takes off the lingerie and lifts her into the spare room. He starts kissing her all over and makes love to her.

When the church is now out, the congregants starts leaving. Thandeka and Catharine remain, waiting outside for him. She has no idea where he has gone. She tries to reach him over the phone, but it takes her to voicemail. An hour passes but he does not appear. Eventually, they board a taxi to Catherine's house. At Catherine's house, August pulled off on a driveway, the front door in the house is open, and the music still plays too loud. Thandiwe's panties, bras and August's pants are scattered on the floor leading to her bedroom. They both proceed into the bedroom, and the shocking scene unfolds before them: August is on top of Thandiwe as they walk in. He scrambles to his feet, dropping his eyes in total shame.

Nothing is prepared to come out of his mouth. He least tries to put on his clothes. However, in one quick moment, Thandeka dodges out of range, hot tears welling down her cheeks; Catherine faints. The following morning, Thandiwe disappears: she is nowhere on sight. She has been nursing a secret; she is two weeks pregnant with August's child.

CHAPTER ELEVEN

The following morning after the incident, Thandeka is locking the front door of her house; she carries with her all the bags she had packed in the middle of the previous night when she had not been able to sleep. She carelessly throws them onto the passenger seat in her car and turns on the ignition key. She slowly drives into the paved driveway, then on the road leading her straight to the hospital where she works. The evening falls, she moves her belongings into her grandmother's house. Sitting across the table from Catherine, Thandeka has no appetite. The events of the previous day are still fresh in her mind. She goes to her bedroom and lies on the bed with her eyes wide open, and her face turned to the wall.

Catherine enters; she has followed her through into the room and now sits down beside her, touches her cheek, which is wet with tears. When she thinks of Thandiwe and August, fresh hot tears gush from her eyes. For August, he is too ashamed, too ashamed to face anyone from Thandeka's family. Nevertheless, during his working hours at the hospital, he arrives at Lady-smith hospital where Thandeka works. He appears in her office and stands in the door. He will not leave her until she talks to him, he tells himself.

'What do you want?' she asks.

'I came to apologize,' he says; and she is silent.

'I'm sorry I hurt you. I'm sorry I lied...'

'What do you want?' she shouts, loudly.

'I beg you to forgive me. I am ready to make any sacrifice for you to come back home. I need you; I'm prepared to do anything, anything!'

'You know, I thought you were the one to keep me happy. I gave you my heart, but you played it all along. I was just a fool, blind and stupid to love you...' She wants to say more of it but her rage cuts her off. She faces him squarely with a frown; he can sense the anger in her, 'get out of my office!'

He wishes he could refuse but something tells him to give her time. He drops his glance, takes few steps back; she closes the door on him, crashes on the floor against the wall and bursts into hot tears. He stands against the door outside her office, hiding his face in his hands, heaves in a point of crying. Then gets to his car and drives off. In secret, he stays in contact with Thandiwe via phone calls. She still wants him, not because she loves him, but it is because of the money she will receive after making love to her. However, for him it seems he has had enough. He knows about her pregnancy, but he is desperate and careless at the same time.

CHAPTER TWELVE

She is in Botswana. A landlocked country in Southern Africa to the west of South Africa. She has come to a country of Tswana origin, a land of different Tswana tribes. Here, everything is different: people live in a different world, in a different atmosphere. She can barely speak SeTswana. She cannot even commerce greetings in Tswana. She is just a stranger who does not have a role in this country. Wait, what is she doing here? What is she up to?

A question without an answer. She tells herself that she wanted to live far from home, disappear from Thandeka, from Catherine. She wants to forget about the Zulu nation; wants to live a new life in a new atmosphere, with new people. Then, here, Tswana is the most spoken native language; there is no Zulu. However, every tribe has its own language that is sometimes very similar to Tswana. A few people speak and understand English in this area. Most of those who understand English live in the urban areas. Each tribal culture plays a different role in the overall Botswana culture; it contributes something special to the culture of Batswana.

Her first month of living here is better. She manages to rent one room in a hotel in ST John Street, Tlokweng, in Gaborone near the railway station, for which she pays five hundred Pula every Sunday. It is not an expensive room it is just affordable. Fortunately, she had saved a bit, from what she earned from August in the previous weeks. She had saved a little to afford food and pay rent on the first month of her stay here. For food, she cooks her meals in a big pot to last her the whole week. She has arranged with a milkman, every morning he leaves a pint of milk at her door. For the rest she buys bread at the corner shop, and saves the change for rental. As for clothes, she has beautiful jackets, skirts, and slacks to wear.

The first five Sunday evenings of the month, she goes into the office of Mr. Ralesolebe, the owner of the hotel, whose office is next to the reception at the basement. She hands the envelope with the rent inside it, Mr. Ralesolebe pours the money out onto his desk and counts it, then writes her a receipt. Ralesolebe is short, and fat. He has dark skin and a big tummy. He seems troublesome. He seems stingy, and greedy.

On this particular Sunday evening, Thandiwe has not paid. The morning of Monday before sunrise, he is at her door. He will not leave, until he receive the envelope. On the first week of the following month, her life becomes a mess, a misery. Whatever that she had saved is finished, and her affair with August is over. She is on her own. Two days after she failed to deliver the envelope, she finds a letter pushed under her door at nine am. Ralesolebe was here, she says to herself. Indeed, she is right. He has written her what he calls a love letter. In the letter, he calls her my friend.

'My dearest friend, with all the love in the world, I must remind you to hand in the package before noon today. Otherwise, you must leave, effective immediately!

Thomas Ralesolebe.'

She was too restless to sleep the previous night. The same morning after receiving the letter, she does not have appetite. At three o'clock the same afternoon she heads for the mountainside and sets off on a long walk, sets off alone on an eight-kilometre loop, walking fast, trying to tire herself out. At five o'clock, she returns. At the gate stands two security guards, both dark, one stocky and the other lanky and tall. As she approaches the hotel gate, she notices Mr. Ralesolebe appearing, he is lifting a mess of clothes into a plastic bag and ties it shut. Two other security men are behind him; they appear with bags and throw them on the pavement on the sidewalks, at the gate, outside the hotel. Then return indoors with Mr. Ralesolebe.

At first, she thinks they are throwing trash; then she realizes they are getting rid of her possessions. All her possessions are outside; her makeup is in the plastic bags. Unless she does something about it, she will spend the night with thugs, in the street. She tries to proceed in, but the security stretches their arms before her, blocking her from passing. 'What's going on here?' she asks.

The tall one murmurs in Tswana, but she has no idea what he is saying. 'I don't know what the hell you're trying to say! I want to go into my hotel room!' she says grimly.

The two men appear to have been waiting for this moment, preparing themselves for it. 'He is telling you that you are not allowed here,' says the short one.

'Says who?' she asks.

'The owner of this place?' says the tall one.

'Why? Where am I supposed to go?'

The two men are silent.

The voice that issues from her throat is thick with rage. 'Answer me!' she says loudly.

The men are still silent, pretending they cannot hear her. Mr. Ralesolebe returns he has come to drop her purse, which carries only her South African passport and her identity book. He passes it to her; she lays a hand on Mr. Ralesolebe's sleeve.

However, Mr. Ralesolebe breaks free, gives her an impatient glare. 'Do you have my money?' he asks Thandiwe.

'Please...'

He cuts her off and throws her purse into her plastic bags. 'Leave my hotel!'

'Please, I beg...' she says, kneeling on the floor.

He is in no state to waste his time for her; he turns and walks away.

'I will telephone the police!' she shouts that he can hear her.

'And say what?' he asks.

'You cannot throw me out without a notice!'

'I wrote to you this morning. What did you do about it?'

She is silent.

'You have to pack your bags and leave. As for the police, if you are too gentle to call them in now, then you should never have bothered with thinking of it in the first place,' says Mr. Ralesolebe, and then disappears.

As dusk settles, she rouses herself, gathers her stuff and leaves the hotel entrance. The first stars are out. Through empty streets, she makes her way to the old age home care, which is seventeen blocks away from the hotel. She knocks at the door; a woman opens the door. She is a bustling woman with black freckles, close-cropped, wiry hair, and no neck. She murmurs something in Tswana. Though Thandiwe does not understand, she begs no pardon.

'My name is Thandiwe, I need a place to sleep,' she says.

'Where do you come from?' asks the woman.

'From South Africa, I was forcedly moved out of my hotel earlier today.'

'You have come to a wrong place, I am afraid.'

'What do you mean?'

'I would like to assist, but this is a place for old people who need
  special care.'
'I know I just need a place to sleep, just one night. Please!'
'Sorry, I can't help you. It is against our policies to allow guests
  to sleep here. I ask for your pardon,' says the woman, and
  slowly closes the door.
From behind her, a group of children pass her on their way home
  from playing soccer. She greets them; they greet her back.
  Children with good manners, child respect is important.
She gathers her things and makes another way to the empty
  parking lot, at the back of the nursing home. Three men are
  eating from a rubbish bin, or two men and a boy. They are
  eating fast, without noticing her. Once the younger one has
  caught her by sight, he saunters off, squarely glancing over her.
  He has been eating a brown loaf of bread, which he found in the
  bin and is holding it with two hands. After a moment, his
  companions join him, gazing over her. She is passing them,
  walking slowly. She is aware of the three men's eyes on her; she
  nods, a greeting, but they do not greet her back.
They all wear baggy clothes and the younger of them wears a
  little yellow sunhat. They are all dark, and slim. They all look
  like trouble. She fastens her pace and vanishes from their sight.
  A block away is a bus station; there is an old bus ahead. She
  lowers her pace, and reaches to it. It has no tyres and
  windshields. Inside when she enters, it has no seats. It is full of
  flyers, advertisements, newspapers. It seems the bus has stood
  there for years, but it has a smell of weed and cigarettes. The
  floor of it smells urine. She puts down her bags, and picks a
  newspaper: it has a picture of a farm, but the text is written in
  SeTswana. Useless, she sits on it and draws her stuff close. She
  unties the plastic bag that has fruit: bananas, apples, and

peaches. It has been a long day, she peels off a banana and eats, eats in the bad smell of urine.

It does not have a good taste; she does not have appetite. Gingerly, she throws it away, and rubs her hands. She draws the bag that carries her clothes; there are two blankets: one brown and one pink. She bought them at a boutique in South Africa.

She takes the blankets out and spreads them on the floor, the brown blanket underneath, the pink on top. She slides under the blanket without removing her clothes. She lies under the blanket with only her head sticking out. After a few minutes, she falls asleep. In the morning, she wakes up minutes before sunrise. Something is wrong, she knows at once. Some of her bags are gone. The plastic bag that held fruit is gone and her makeup has disappeared. In fact, all her bags, except for the one that held her clothes and her purse, have disappeared.

She gets up, gathers her remaining things and steps out of the bus. In the street, there is a smell of burning meat. A mist hangs over the town; people rub their hands, stamp their feet, and curse. Street vendors start arriving, by car, by taxi, on foot. Almost everyone is arriving with boxes of flowers, pockets of potatoes, onions, cabbage. Two women who arrived early are sitting on canvas stools.

They drink coffee from a thermos flask, waiting for their first customers. They sell potatoes, onions, bottled goods, preservatives, dried fruit, and packets of buchu tea, honeybush tea, and herbs. Those who just arrived are unpacking their goods. Most of the vendors here are women, staid, solid. There is one old odd woman. She is wearing men's blue suit and a garish yellow shirt. Thandiwe is pacing, passing them, watching and running her eyes on them. She is not expecting these people to feel pity for her or to offer their help, is she?

Next on the left are three African women with carrots, onions, butter to sell; also, from a bucket with a wet cloth over it, soup-bones and fat cakes. Next to the three women are three men who were eating from a rubbish bin the previous day. They are selling makeup, perfume, soap, and towels. Like other vendors, they have bananas, apples and peaches to sell. Customers cluster around them, seem buying from the three men. The two of the men stand at a distance, talking, drinking, and laughing, while the boy is busy with the customers. Thandiwe paces towards them. There are many pairs of shoulders to fight past ('Excuse me ... Excuse me'), she notices the boy clearly; he is a kid who cannot be more than twelve. Like all his companions, he still wears the same baggy clothes, but today he wears a clean black cap, which looks like hers.

Soon when the boy notices her, he saunters off and re-joins his companions. At once things fall into place. She knows all the goods they are selling, knows them intimately. The three men have robbed her, and have been selling her stuff. Already, they have sold her new brushes, matte lips, eyeliners, face powder, her foundations and concealers. What is she going to do about it?

'What are you doing?' she asks the boy.

The boy is silent; she looks at their goods; he has sold some of her makeup and towels. 'You-thugs!' she says grimly, 'This is my stuff!'

At once, she has received almost everyone's attention. She picks one of the towels left, 'You stole my stuff, and you are selling it!' she repeats.

There is a disapproving murmur from the onlookers. 'These are my towels,' she indicates them.

'These are all my things; these men stole my things. I want them back, all of them!' she says to the crowd as they are clustering around her, pushing, jostling, and interjecting.

'I'm coming with the police!' she says, turning; the crowd gives way before her. She murmurs angrily before she can reach the edge of the crowd finds her way out, and emerges into the street.

Barely an hour later has she returned with two police officers: a constable and a seargant, in a police van. She is the first to jump out of the vehicle, and leads the way to the spot where three men were. She hopes they did not disappear. There is hell to pay for them; they cannot get away with it. Indeed, they did not

disappear. However, when she arrives, they are only selling
fruits. Either the rest of the stuff has been sold out, or they hid
it somewhere. All street vendors mind their own business.

'Here they are,' she says, indicating them. In front of them, she
plants herself. 'I want my stuff,' she says. The three men,
including the boy, seem not startled. They have planned for this
moment, planned for this scene. They look through one
another, and shake their heads with puzzled faces.

All eyes turn toward her, toward the stranger. She does not mind
the attention. Let them know I am still here, she thinks; let
them know I am not afraid of them. In addition, if that spoils
their dirty businesses, so be it. 'I said I want my stuff!' she
repeats.

Again, from the vendors comes angry murmurings. 'Who are
you?' asks the woman wearing men's blue suit and a garish
yellow shirt.

'I'm the owner of the stuff that they were selling here, and who
the hell are you?'

'What stuff?' asks the woman again.

'Don't make me a fool. We both know what these thugs were
selling here,' she turns to the police officers, 'Ask them where
my stuff is, they know it.'

The onlookers are still disapproving. 'Enough!' interjects one of
the police officers, the male one. Then turns to the three men,
talking fast in Tswana. Then turns again to Thandiwe. 'They say
do not know what you talking about. They say they only saw
you today when you stepped out of the bus and came straight to
them and accused them of stealing your fruits,' he says to her.

'They were selling perfumes, makeup, manicures. Ask everyone,
they saw it!'

From behind, the police officer puts her hand on Thandiwe's
holder. 'Mam,' she says, 'These people might have robbed you.
However, there is no proof. We cannot arrest them.'
'But they stole from me!'
The female officer turns to the three men and says something in
Tswana, but the old woman in a yellow shirt interjects,
speaking to the officer in Tswana.
'What is she saying?' asks Thandiwe.
'I was asking the boys where they got the fruits. But the lady over
there says she gave them the fruits this morning.'
'This is rubbish.'
'There is nothing we can do,' says the police officer.
'She is defending them; can't you see it?'
'Mam, we can argue all day. Nevertheless, we do not have proof.
These men are homeless, it is not possible to investigate them,'
says the police officer.
'This is not right; you can't leave without even trying to find a
resolution.'
'I'm sorry,' says the police officer, then turning to his colleague,
'Let's go.'
The officers return to their vehicle and drive off. The crowd is
still staring at her; with a stoned face, she turns and disappears
from the scene. At nine pm. The same evening, the street is
empty, she returns to the old bus. What a long day. She opens
her bag that is full of her fancy clothes, and takes out the
blankets. She spreads them on the floor: the brown blanket
underneath, the pink on top. She slips inside them and falls
asleep. At midnight, she opens her eyes; there are visitors.
There are three of them: one is on the right, one on the left,
and the other one is in front of her. The one in front is a bit
short. She knows the face; it is one of the three men. Actually,

it is the boy, the youngest of the three. He is carrying an axe. She is in no state to wait to comprehend this; quickly, she scrambles to her feet and fight her way past the boy and runs into the street. If she left, her bag of clothes behind, the strangers will not bother to chase her, run behind her. On the contrary, they will let her run on her own.

Two kilometres from the bus station, she reaches to a farm rich of fruit and vegetables. She has no idea who it belongs to, no idea the name of the place, but she is heaving badly —she decides to take a rest. She would like to eat, but she does not have appetite. An hour later, she falls asleep, lying on potato beds. At 6 am. The farm workers start arriving, they carry shovels. She is dead asleep to pay heed. She wakes up when someone is murmuring something. It is a man; he is carrying a shovel, wearing an overall. He is standing at her legs. The man is speaking, but Thandiwe has no idea what he is saying. Her eyes flit nervously across him as he speaks. Once he has finished speaking, orating, he pauses, waits, and allows silence to develop, a silence that Thandiwe ought to fill with her comment, but she does not; he says something again in Tswana. Thandiwe seems not to understand what he says. 'What do you speak?' he finally asks in English.

'Zulu,' she says.

'Oh! I was asking; who are you?'

'Thandiwe.'

The man can see all the nervousness in her eyes. 'Relax,' he says. 'What are you doing on this farm?'

A pause before she speaks. 'I don't have a place to stay.'

'Where do you come from?'

'South Africa.'

'I know you're from South Africa. I want to know where you
first lived before you ended up here.'
'I lived in a hotel, downtown, near the train station.'
'And what happened?'
She is silent. A pity, he can see it in her eyes, her story makes
sense. The man looks around; no one can see them. Then, to
Thandiwe: 'Can you walk?' he asks.
She nods a yes.
'Come,' he gives her a hand to scramble. Then takes her for a
walk, he is walking her down through the shrubs. One hour
thirty minutes from the farm, they are reaching their
destination, the village of Maratadiaba on the St George's road
outside Gaborone. The man's house is at the middle of a
winding dirt track some miles in the middle of the village. The
house is surrounded by corrals. Hens are almost all over the
yard, laying eggs everywhere. It is a farmhouse painted white,
with iron roof and a covered stoep. Old rusty Zink, matrass,
and wood mark the front boundary; the rest of the front is dust
and gravel. The house is large, dark, with no electricity and,
water. He unlocks the back door and enters. 'Come in,' he
says.
Poor Thandiwe follows. Inside, the house is just as she had
imagined it would be; rubbishy furniture, cowbells on the floor,
toilet papers scattered on the floor, cats everywhere underfoot,
the smell of cat and dog urine greets them.
'Sit here,' he says, indicating the sofa and disappears into the
other room. Thandiwe will sit, as long as she receives the help
that she needs.
After a moment, he appears with a jar of water and a tumbler.
Surprisingly, the jar and the tumbler are clean. He pours water
in the jar and passes it to her. She drinks without inhibition.

'You want more?' he asks when she is done.

She nods a yes; he pours again, passes the tumbler; puts the jar on the table, then returns into the room. When he returns, he is carrying a plate filled with sandwiches, and a cup of tea. He offers her tea. She is hungry: she wolfs down eight blocks-like slices of bread with jam and peanut butter.

'You want more?' he asks again, once she is done.

She has had enough; she shakes her head. 'Thank you,' she says.

He picks the empty plates and and returns into the room, which Thandiwe already knows is a kitchen. A few minutes later, he returns. 'Follow me,' he says.

He is leading her into the bathroom. He has run water for her in the big, old-fashioned, cast-iron bathtub. In the bathroom, there is a tablet of bath soap and a pile of towels. 'Wear this when you are done,' he passes her pyjamas. When she finishes bathing, she returns to the smelly living room. She has her arms folded across her breasts. She is in her borrowed pyjamas. The man, the stranger offering to assist another stranger, is sitting on the smelling sofa waiting for her. She comes; sits across him, on the sofa that has a mat of pieces of toilet paper and sand cakes on it.

'Thank you again,' she says.

'How are you doing?'

She shrugs.

'What's your plan?'

'I don't know I don't have any.'

Her nose drips; he finds her a tissue.

'This is not an easy thing to talk about,' he says, 'but where is your family?'

She gathers herself and blows her nose. The smell is not good. She does not meet his eyes. She does not wish to reply.

'What was your name again?' he repeats.

'Thandiwe.'

'Why did you come to this country?'

She shakes her head.

'If you need help, I advise you to respond to my questions,' he says. 'Are we clear?'

'Yes.'

'Do you have family around?'

'No.'

He is silent, gathering his thoughts. Then 'May I ask about your life in South Africa?'

She does not dignify the question with a reply.

He gets up. If she chooses to be irritable, then he can be irritable too. 'I'm sorry I asked,' he says. 'What are your plans for today?'

'I don't have anything in mind,' she says. 'Perhaps to go back to the farm, or to the street.'

'And then? Go on as before?'

'Yes.'

'Be sensible. Things have changed. You can't just pick up where you left off.'

'I have nowhere else to go.'

He pauses, stares at her. Their eyes meet. He sees all the beauty in her eyes. A real beauty she must have been in her day. Her features remain stiff, though she has been sleeping in the street. In the past years, the beauty of women has always fascinated him.

The truth is he has always had much of an eye for women. Much of an eye for all of them, including little girls. It is not surprising that he might be falling for the beauty of the Zulu girl.

'You can stay,' he says, 'Because it's not a good idea. It's not safe.'

'I don't know what to say. Thank you very much!'
He nods with an overwhelmed smile, and leaves. What does the
  smile mean? Is he really having an eye on her, on Thandiwe?
At evening, he settles her on a matress, in the spare room that
  smells of cats. No lights, she uses a candle, which she blows off
  when she sleeps. She allows him to kiss her good night on the
  forehead, and then leaves her to herself. When he returns half
  an hour later, she is in a dead sleep, fully clothed. What a
  surprising ease she falls asleep in a house of a stranger, a man
  whose name she does not even know.

CHAPTER FOURTEEN

Hours before the sun rise. He is ready for the day at the farm, fully dressed: overall, and boots. Cautiously he switches on his flashlight, taps on Thandiwe's door, pushes it open and enters. There is a chair by the bedside; he sits. She is lying with her face turned to the other side of the wall. The sheet is drawn up to her chin. His senses tell him she is awake. What is he doing? He is watching over a stranger, wishing her a good morning.

'Good morning,' he says.

There is a pause before she speaks, then turn to him. 'Hey.'

'How are you feeling?' he asks.

She shrugs.

'Do you need anything?'

She shakes her head mutely.

'I'm going to the farm,' he says. 'There is water in the kettle, in the kitchen if you want to bath. You can boil it if you want. There is breakfast in the pot, on the stove, help yourself. See you soon.'

'Wait. You didn't tell me your name.'

'Timothy,' he says.

'Thanks, Timothy. You are so kind.'

After he has gone off to work, she gets up. In the kitchen, he has made breakfast of porridge; sugar is in the old-fashioned iron mug, which is left on the kitchen table. She will eat, as long as she is hungry. Four weeks pass. It makes it two months since she has left South Africa. She does not forget that she is pregnant. As long as she is having August's child, she will not return home.

She does not have a wish for it. Timothy is aware of it, Thandiwe has told him about it. However, she did not mention the story of herself and August, or the reason she came to this country. For the time she has lived with Timothy, she has also discovered some things about him. In fact, Timothy has spoken many things about himself with Thandiwe. He owns the farm, the one he where met Thandiwe. He owns cattle, goats, sheep, donkeys, hens. However, he does not have a wish to sell them; he wants to keep them for a living, it is his culture. He is not poor —he can afford to buy anything he would like. He has bought Thandiwe clothes, makeup, shoes, and perfumes.

He is seven times divorced, with no children. In the past years, he had turned abusive, violent to any woman that he married. He had affairs with wives of his neighbours, friends, and even his relatives, he says.

Now that Thandiwe knows about Timothy, she has begun to like him for his kindness. However, because she has no love for any kind of man, she has toyed with the idea that she makes no impressions on them. Men that she regards to live in poverty, with poor background are attracted by her looks but she disdains their love proposals.

Timothy has become one of them, he would like to have an affair with her, but for Thandiwe, Timothy is not fit to be a lover to her. His relationship with her will always be of friends, or rather be of a stranger offering to assist another stranger, out of kindness.

She only entertains poor men because she wants to earn a living. She would like to get help from them, as much as she needs Timothy to help her. Nonetheless, from Timothy's pocket, she is able to eat well. There is no rent to pay, no child to maintain, no bill, few responsibilities for him. For Thandiwe's unborn child, he has arranged for Thandiwe to meet with Jualine twice a week at the hospital. Jualine is a nurse, a young Indian woman. She works at Molope health care. It is not a public hospital, but a private nursing home. She has to check the condition of the baby, ensure that it lives in a healthy condition. For the session with the nurse, Timothy will have to pay 1800 Pula. For each session he gives Thandiwe 2500 Pula, she will pay the hospital 1800 Pula, and spend the rest on her reasons. However, Thandiwe keeps the money to herself, and dodges the appointment.

Of course, Timothy was brutal in the past year. Nevertheless, he, himself has a strong belief that he has changed. He has managed to convince Thandiwe to believe it too. However, things change. On Friday in the evening, Thandiwe is in her borrowed bedroom changing her clothes, about to put on pyjamas. There is a knock at the door. It is Timothy. Without invitation, he enters; she is naked. A moment she did not expect to come, the intruder who throws himself upon her surprises her.

However, she did not expect this to happen, she must not make any effort to refuse, restrain him. She would rather avail herself because there is nothing to stop him. She allows him to put his lips on her vagina. She does not feel anything for him. Nevertheless, she presses his head tighter to her part, the part that will make a man die for it.

She does not want to kiss him nor touch his body. Then, perhaps, he can or has already noticed her strained face. Perhaps he has noticed she does not like him as much as he thinks, but he does not want to stop, and she does not say anything to discourage him directly.

After that he makes love to her, she scrambles to her feet and gathers her stuff, trying to disappear into the bathroom. But he is not yet satisfied. The mood for it wolfs him. He grabs her and makes love to her one more time. Despite that, she does not sense him in a fully sexual appetite; he feels a surge of joy and a full desire. Whatever she gets does not bring her joy; she remembers how she used to play with her sister in the days she was at home. Sometimes when she thinks about it, her tears roll down her cheeks and hit the floor. When it is done she stays up until midnight, with no appetite. It was not rape, not quite that, but undesired to the core. She has been enjoying his offers. She is a woman, living in a house of a man who has had many divorces, a stranger that always had affairs with wives of neighbours. What did she expect from him? Did she expect to live in a world of milk and honey? Obviously, he loved her; he could not resist her. For all he has been doing for her, now she must pay the price: that is the common way of payment for women. She sheds tears of torment. The tears flow down her face; her hands shake. The place is not safe for her.

The man that was like Jesus to her has turned a devil; she cannot guarantee a good life with him. Otherwise, she will end up like the women that he is divorced. She might die at his hands, she tells herself. She has saved enough from dodging the session with the nurse. The same night, at midnight, she packs her bags and disappears. No need to judge her, she is running for her life, for the life of the unborn baby as well.

CHAPTER FIFTEEN

She hides herself in Francistown, 432, 7 kilometres from Gaborone. She rents a flat, for which she pays 1000 Pula a month. She has bought food, enough to last her the rest of the month. She still has enough to survive for a while. It amazes her that August liked giving her presents; he enjoyed her pleasure, which she thought it was quite ineffective. No emotion, no need to cry. On her previous birthday, he had given her an enameled bracelet. At night, she thinks of him, coming to her, coming for a reckless fucking life. Then, from now on, she will be on her own. There will be no bliss in her life! She says marveling at herself in the mirror. She decides on doing something. The next morning she visits the most potent healer in the Tati village, near the town. Before she knocks on the door, he has already noticed her.

'Come in,' he says. 'Take off your shoes.'

She obeys and proceeds in, then sits down on the floor.

'How can I help you?'

At first, she is silent; she does not believe in this life. A life of spiritual practices, spiritual practices that change a human life. She has never been a true believer of miracles even in South Africa she seldom went to church. Spiritual affairs have nothing to satisfy her. 'My name is Thandi. I have been facing problems these days, financially,' she says afterwards.

'What do you want me to do for you?'

She is silent again, doubtful to speak. Then, 'I need you to help me earn an income.'

He clears his throat, gathers himself and takes a deep breath. 'It's
an easy task,' he says.
She begins to free herself. 'OK!'
'But it depends on how you pay.'
'With what money?'
He is silent; she ought to mind her words.
'How much do you want?' she repeats.
'It's not about money. It's about human blood.'
'Human blood?'
'Yes. Kill a person and give his blood to us as a sacrifice. Then
you will be more than welcome to claim everything you want,
anytime.'
She pauses, and swallows hard. She does not know what to say,
does not even have a word in her mouth. She remains tongue-
tied; he does not take an effort to help her. 'Isn't there any
other way to pay you?'
'I would have mentioned it.'
'Do you mind if I bring you the person and you do the job?'
'Lady, I'm not the one looking for help. You have to do it
yourself, for your own benefit.'
He passes a powder wrapped in a small plastic. 'Mix it with food,
and give it to the person you want to see dead.'
'I don't know a lot of people here.'
'I see you are pregnant.'
'So?'
'Bring the baby as a sacrifice.'
'Are you mad? It's not yet even born!'
'If you need help, eat the powder I gave you. The baby will come
out within two days, but it will be dead. Therefore, you will
bring it here and I will do the ritual. You will do it only if you
want to see your life very different.'

She tends to be deadly desperate. She waits a few days before she
makes her mind. She has never had a child before. However,
once she has made up her mind there is nothing to hold her
back. She eats the powder, and a day passes. The baby dies in
the hut of the healer. The same day, he begins with the ritual in
a perennial river, Tati River. Tati River is a tributary of the
Shashe River, which in turn is a tributary of the Limpopo River.
The river flows through Francistown, where it is joined by the
Ntshe (or Inchwe) River from the left. It is a few miles outside
the village. She is cleansed with the baby's blood at midnight.
'How long is this going take?' She asks.
'Relax, just for little while.'
She spends a more than a week living with the healer, at his hut
eating the baby's raw flesh for eight full days; drinking its blood
every morning when she wakes up to quench her thirst. It is
part of the ritual. She has a duty to do it. The following day is
the final day. An unfortunate scene; the healer dies. Her life
becomes miserable. She begins to hate tradition with a passion.
Her life is messed up. This is retributive punishment itself. At
this point, it would have been better to kill herself. She thinks
about going back home. Nevertheless, she is ashamed of herself.
Does she regret it? To a certain degree, she regrets running
away in the first place. She wishes she had never slept with
August. However, it is her desire to sleep with every man who
crosses her path.

CHAPTER SIXTEEN

Many young women of her age have completed their university studies. Some of them live with their husbands, some have children, but for herself, she earns no living. She lives without any source of income. She is not married, does not even have a kid. Then, she does not hesitate to have an affair with anyone. She would like to have an affair with any rich man because no one knows her whereabouts. There is no sign that she has given birth to a child. Is she happy with that? By her standards, she believes she is. She wears vermillion makeup. Her life seems to change now. However, not to the extent she wants it to be.

Back in South Africa Thandeka is still gripped by depression. She is constrained by Christianity at the same time. Sunday morning, she is at her church, sitting next to Catherine. Grandchild and her grandmother, they come to church together, sit side by side. This time the pastor preaches about pure love. He reads aloud:

'You should trust one another in your relationship. As his wife, make sacrifices for him; make sacrifices for her as her husband too. With these spiritual attributes in your marriage, your relationship shall never fall apart. Depend on him as a wife and he will depend on you as a husband. Do not hold grudges against one another, even if he has made a mistake. Otherwise, your marriage will never last long. Do not be an object of hate on the basis that someone has hurt you,' he says.

"Repent, then, and trust God, so that your sins may be wiped out, that times of refreshing may come from the lord" That is in the book of Acts 3:19," the pastor adds.

Many times, Thandeka lets the bible lead, guide her. She uses it to judge herself. The commandments in the book of life are very important they do not escape her: they are not just spiritual rules; they help her build her temperament. Often assist with her moral values. Though the incident has pissed her, she does not prefer hate to complacency.

August is still a husband to her. Regardless of what happens, she will always find a way back to him, love him as much as before. In addition, she does not wish to hold up a grudge against him for the whole of her life. With her attributes of life, she somehow finds herself prepared to make a way for him into her life again. Things have already begun to settle for her. Monday morning, she goes into his office, at the surgery. August has disappeared; he is nowhere to be found. She returns again the following morning, and the morning of Wednesday.

When she comes, she stands, waiting at the door. However, there is no sign of him. For a whole week, he does not come to work. He is not even at his house. She has been hoping for the best to come, but the best that comes to her is the worst, worst of all. Perhaps she ought to forget about him, forget that she has ever met him. Otherwise, it will destroy her innocent being. On Friday at noon, the hospital she works at is closed. She has offered to help her grandmother in the house. Despite the pain she feels inside, she tries to be easy on her, she is merely an innocent old soul that needs peace, dignity. She has no intention to strain her.

As for Catherine herself, she also tries to spend her daytime hours off her besides leaving her to think alone. However, she is convinced to make a confession, say something to Thandeka. It is something that will change the life of someone. It will bring and sink her life into a state of disgrace from which it will not be easy to lift herself. Moreover, the good part of it is the fact that she does not murmur against it. The Lord, the Messiah who swayed out the secret of Thandiwe and August has returned. He has now come to destroy Catherine. The time that was spared for her prejudice has now arrived. Months before they discovered the affair of August and Thandiwe, the secret that she has been bearing for her whole life has been haunting her. She is too restless to sleep at night. She has decided to let everything out, let Thandeka know about it for the time being. After the work in the garden, Catherine returns indoors. When she appears again, Thandeka is outside on the veranda, lying on a picnic blanket. She is lying with her eyes open. She first says her name, and then mumbles something in Zulu.

'I'm not sleeping,' replies Thandeka.

'Do you have a moment to speak?'

She nods, wakes up and sits.

Then Catherine sits down on the blanket, draws herself close. She has brought a photo album. On the top of it is a photograph of a man, neither too old nor too young. He is wearing a perfect-sized black suit. She whispers again in Zulu, and then passes the photograph. 'This is the man you always wanted to know about. He is your father, Themba Khumalo.'

For the moment, Thandeka draws a close look over it. The man took after Catherine: skin color, the forehead, eyes, and chubby cheekbones. She smiles. The photograph that follows is of a woman. 'She is the woman he was married to,' says Catherine.

She contemplates it; she is wearing a wedding dress with gaudy jewelry. She is a stranger; she appears to be a lost woman who left nothing for her children. Nothing, not even a feature that shows she is a mother to her. 'Is it my mother?' she asks.

This is the moment. The secret that has been haunting her life has to come out. However, before she speaks, she thinks, deeply in the soil of memories.

She pauses. Blank incomprehension to this moment, the scene. She has gone too far too fast. Memories flood back: the moment the girl's parents left. She remembers how the girls were born, she thinks of the stupid sound of it. The vision of it is suddenly too old-fashioned, queer. In this respect, she continues to think, her decision has been stupid. She, herself, is a good woman who takes care to her grandchildren. Despite this, if she mentions many things about the girl's parents, she, herself is still struggling to settle with the story of her husband. It will destroy her, she tells herself. It will destroy her relationship with her own grandchild. Although she decided by myself, without being pushed, she changes her mind. For a second, she has decided to go slack, let the secret die within herself for the duration of her life, like a gazelle when the jaws of the predator close on its neck.

The pause has taken too long. For the first time she looks up, her eyes meet Catherine's eyes and in a flash sees all. Uncomfortably, Catherine drops her glance. Then, now is not the perfect time for it, she does not tell anyone about it. This secret needs to remain hidden. Even Thandeka does not have to know about it. Nevertheless, the worst, the darkest part would be that Catherine engaged something strange in her life that now has affected, or, is affecting her grand children's lives. However, the secret has to be buried with her; if the girls have to find out, they will find out from someone else, not her. It would be too simple. The truth she suspects is something far more — she will have to cast around for the word - anthropological, something it would take months to find the underlying cause of, months of patient, unhurried conversation with dozens of relatives.

'She was your mother,' she says afterwards. Nevertheless, what she will say is a lie, a total untruthful story. 'But she has passed on.'

'What happened?'

'She was having affairs with husbands of her colleagues. She was sleeping with my husband too. When it was known, they burnt her.'

'What?'

'They set fire on her, alive.'

Her face is stiff as she fights off tears.

She draws her closer. My daughter, she thinks, my dearest child. The atmosphere of it is not good, it has never been good, and it will never be good for her. She cuts the story, cuts it and tosses it aside. She does not dismiss the idea that the truth always has a way of coming out. She has learnt it from August and Thandiwe. The ones who know the Lord Messiah, and obey his rules will be saved, delivered from evil. However, the ones who know Him and do the opposite of it will never find peace. They will be haunted by their sins, and will be destroyed. She out to remember this, keep it in her head.

CHAPTER SEVENTEEN

August has disappeared to live with his parents. He has returned to London, the city where he comes from. He did not run away, he just returned home —nothing wrong with that. There is nothing wrong with a person who chooses to go back to live in his country if he does not enjoy living as a foreigner in another country. He went to South Africa to study Medicine and become a medical doctor, not to be caught up in a relationship with some African women, twin sisters who would both like to be with him.

He might be passionate about Thandeka, but London: a city of love, city of art; always will come first. Nevertheless, coming to live in London, does it mean he has left South Africa for good? Is he leaving everything, his marriage, his career, and his properties behind? Is he sorry for Thandeka? Certainly, he is sorry Thandeka is innocent.

She does not deserve whatever that has happened. However, the real question is what was his motive for leaving South Africa? Did he perhaps leave in order that he stays away from her? Is leaving South Africa going to help him forget about her? If no, then was it difficult to stop playing around and try by himself to find his own way of telling her that he was too cowardly to have affair with her sister? Is he too much of a coward to say that to her face? What are his true thoughts anyway? These questions cannot be answered; he himself cannot even answer them too. However, is he happy to be here? He is not certain about it. Nevertheless, his senses tell him he is not happy. Some days he feels happy, even privileged, to be living with his parents. On other days, he feels differently. He is married to a beautiful African woman, a woman whose pleasure is enough to make him happy. It does not make him happy for the woman that he loves to be living alone.

He is in England, in London with his parents; they have jobs, proper jobs for which they are paid four times his salary, better than mere working in South Africa as a medical doctor. He has escaped South Africa. Everything is going well with his parents, they own a penthouse at River Themes, London, and he ought to be happy with that. Then, as the weeks pass, he finds himself more and more miserable. He has attacks of sorrow, which he beats off with difficulty. Three weeks after he left the Zulu state, things that he was hoping to settle with do not go according to his plans. At nine pm, in the blue pyjamas that he has brought from South Africa, he is lying on a bed in his Parent's penthouse. Though he has covered his feet with a cushion, they remain icy.

In the middle of the night, he awakes up in a state of the utmost clarity. He has had a vision: Thandeka has spoken to him, her words — 'Why are you doing this to me? Why don't you want me to live as happy as you are?' - Still echo in his ears. In the vision Thandeka stands, hands folded, wet hair combed back, in a field of white light. Quickly, he gets up. It was a dream, a nightmare, he notices.

As long as it is a dream, it is not important, he says to himself. He tries to get back to sleep, but cannot. It must be that he is always thinking about it. He will have to stop thinking about it, forget it at once. However, it bothers him. He is not in state to call himself happy if Thandeka is not happy. She is the first woman he liked in his life. Besides, she is a young innocent woman who does not deserve any of this. Indeed, why is he doing this to Thandeka? He is not happy to be here. The figure of the woman in his mind stays before him. 'Why did you do this to me?' cries Thandeka, her words clear, ringing, immediate. Is it possible that Thandeka's soul could have left her body and come to him, follow him to London?

What is the point of coming all the way from Pietermaritzburg to London if he would like to be with her? It is not a lie that he is ashamed of himself, not entirely. From Monday to Monday, he has nothing to do; he spends his time reading every book he finds in his father's study room. Reading has become a tool for him to break loneliness. He spends Saturdays in bookshops, galleries, museums, cinemas. On Sunday, he reads a new book in his room that he has bought from a bookshop, and then goes to a film or for a walk. Though he tries all he can to break loneliness, his Sunday evenings are the worst.

The loneliness that he usually manages to keep at bay sweeps over him, loneliness indistinguishable from the low, grey, wet weather of London. The city of Art cannot be fed on deprivation alone, on longing, loneliness. There must be intimacy, passion, love as well. For the fact that he is not happy to come back to London, he loses weight. He has no appetite for anything. His diet is unvarying: apples, oats porridge, bread and cheese, and spiced sausages called chipolatas, which he fries over the cooker. He prefers chipolatas to real sausages because they do not need to be refrigerated. Unless he returns to South Africa, he will live his life like this; he will never have his own peace until Thandeka finds her own first.

CHAPTER EIGHTEEN

Sometimes life is more challenging to live beyond other aspects, and Thandiwe falls into this category. It has more to do with the sense that peradventure she has lost sight of the person she could have been from the beginning. Nevertheless, it does not mean she has forever lost the opportunity to gain that personality. Although she has left South Africa for a while, she is still new in Botswana; she still does not earn a salary. Her entire savings, which she has brought with her from Gaborone, amount to Two thousand Pula. It will not last her for long; she must find a job at once. On Saturday, she visits the offices of the Francistown Bread and Breakfast and enters her name on a list of relief chefs, chefs ready to fill vacancies at short notice. Before sunset, she is at Galo Mall, looking for a job in every space of the mall. When it gets dark, she walks out, exiting through the front entrance of the shopping Centre. A black Audi A7 sport-back pulls up at a parking zone, opposite her. As the door opens, a young classy man shows up. He slides out and slams the car door, walks on a path towards her. Just my type, she says to herself, because she ought to know who she is. He has caught all her attention; it gives her pride, surrounding herself with people like him. Not because she takes pleasure in them, but for the benefit of the bill they will pay.

He smiles at her. He is tall, fit and has a brown skin. He catches up with her.

'Hey,' he says weaning off his sunglasses.

She smiles back, bobbing her head, her smile sly rather than shy.
'Hello,' she responds.
His name is Gill Martins, when he introduces himself. She
introduces herself with her middle name, Gladness. They
exchange a few words; suddenly he takes her to his car and
drives away.
He takes her to his house, 2024 Block10, Kazungula road, two
kilometres from St Patrick. The destination is in the Kazungula
mountainside. Two cars of the Mercedes Benz family are parked
outside the house. The house is large and brightened by its own
lights. It is a nine-bedroom house built with jasper-stones
outside. He ushers her in.
The inside of it is not as she had imagined it would be; it is softly
lit. There is fancy furniture, and appliances, even the floor is
made of an African wooden-tile. It holds a pleasant smell of
fresh air. What a fancy style of living!
'Is this your house?' she asks.
'Yes.'
'Who are you living with?'
'I'm alone.'
'Aren't you married?'
'No.' He leads her into the kitchen, which is also neat, but the
design of it is different: the paint of it is brown matching with
its furniture. 'Want a drink?' he asks.
'No, thank you.'
'Just one round.'
'No.'
'Come on, one glass.'
A pause first, then, 'Fine. One glass.'
He offers her a glass of Pineapple-champagne.
'So you said you are from South Africa?' he asks.

'Yes'

'Can you tell me more about it?'

'What do you want to know?'

'Anything.'

'Anything like what?'

'Your life there, your parents…'

She takes a sip and sets the glass back on the table.

'I have to get going before it gets dark,' she says.

'We just got here. You can stay …'

'No. I have a lot to do at home,' she says grimly.

They just met the same day; he has no duty to make an effort to detain her. 'Ok, I will take you home,' he says.

'Thank you.'

She waits until he finishes his glass, and picks up his car keys from the table. 'Come let's go,' he says opening the door. In the car, she is quiet, so he tries to put her at ease. 'You're so amazing,' he says.

'Really?'

'Yes…' he cuts himself short; he thinks he might bore her. However, she smiles and says nothing.

He draws up before her apartment block: 'Thanks for the ride,' she says opening the door. Before she is conscious of it, he has clutched her by hand pulling her back in the car.

He has given her no warning: he is on her, his tongue slides into her mouth. She does not wriggle out. In return, she gives him a steady regard.

'I am sorry for that…' he says.

'Does it really matter?'

'What do you mean?'

'You feel so nice, so sweet. I'd like more of that next time.'

She slides out of the car and leaves. 'I'm glad there will be next time,' he says as he turns the key and the car surges away. He does not know much, but he is mildly smitten with her. At work, he tries to take a break, goes into the bathroom, pees, and washes his hands in the basin. There he looks into the mirror, but the image of the girl, in his mind, appears in his reflection.

He believes she is so lovely, very special. If he had had a chance to love her, he would have done it long ago, he imagines. He would take pleasure in her, though it would fall, perhaps he would do anything to make it work. For what he knows of pleasure: love is sincere, it can buy fulfilment, and it practices hospitality.

No matter what passes, he would be in joyful hope, and faithful in love. Is Thandiwe the first woman that he is madly in love with? Unbelievably, he has been married, twice, and twice divorced. The divorces had happened because the women he was married to had affairs with other men. He does not have time for whores, immature women. They are not his kind, he doubts they will ever be. Then, he has never loved a woman the way he loves her. No woman has ever made him feel the way he does. Therefore, now he is no longer concerned about anything, he focuses his attention on how bad he wants her on his side. The feeling of seeing her every day is something that will never escape his head; he often never wants to let it go.

CHAPTER NINETEEN

It often annoys to talk about her life in South Africa. She prefers not to mention it to anyone; this is her privacy, her life. She has no duty to share the story of her life with anyone. For a few minutes, she sits on the bed reading a comic book. A message from Gill clicks on her cellphone: 'How about dinner tonight?' she reads out. Then grows quiet at him, working through something else in her mind. After an hour, he receive a response from her: 'Tomorrow? I'm busy tonight.'

The following day he sets a calamari dinner and throws a Cîroc Champagne and chocolate croissants for dessert. Unfortunately, she does not appear as she had promised. She is in her bedroom, lying in bed. Tears fall on her pillow as she thinks of her child that she killed, she has murdered an innocent soul. Does she regret it? Perhaps. He opts something different. Unvited, he knocks at her door the same night. She comes to open, her face is swollen, her eyes reddish. She is tying the belt of a dressing gown that is clearly wet with tears. 'It's you,' she remarks.

'Can I come in?'

'If you want.'

'You promised you would come.'

A long pause as she ushers him in. There is a hint of depression in his face, but she does not say anything though, nor does he seem to care. The inside of the apartment is a bit dark as lights are turned off.

'I really find it difficult to understand why it should be a big deal for two people to catch up for dinner together. You ask me questions and I give you answers; I ask you questions you do the same!' he repeats.

'We just met a few days ago. Why is it supposed to be a big deal if I don't want to see you?'

'Because I love you,' he says without thinking to himself. 'I loved you from the very beginning.'

After a while, he feels his breath begin to relax. A soft pop as his lips separate, and the gentlest of his voice as he continues.

'Lately I have been thinking much about you. I long for the feeling you gave me the day I first saw you.'

She is captivated. It does not make her forget about her depression. She still struggles to sleep at night when she thinks about it. She would lie in bed and press a pillow on her breasts. In her imaginations, she sees a baby face that she cannot recognize. The pain reflected in her face is nothing; it does not even reflect half of what she feels inside her. In the middle of the night, she throws things away, crying trying to figure it out. She realizes that she takes every piece of the blame. Unfortunately, she can do nothing about it. There is no way she can turn back what happened. She closes the chapter.

CHAPTER TWENTY

As for him, he does not mind giving her his fullest attention. Every morning he sends a short message or e-mail keeping her on her toes. She still loves surprises, so he spoils her with random gifts to satisfy her. Nevertheless, he wants to be intimate with her. He invites her for a film, for a home cinema at his house.

She agrees to come; he spends the whole day in bed and wakes up when the sun sets.

He prepares as he has arranged. At this moment, she arrivess at his house. On a sofa, they watch a thriller. She is leaning on him while he works and runs his fingers through her hair. He contemplates her; a beautiful girl in a beautiful world, he is blessed to have her. He is watching over his pretty girl, celebrating the moment of his life with the new angel that has been brought to him by God. She enjoys the quiet of the late evening in the living room. It does not surprise him that she is enjoying his company; he is a creature of passion. He would like to make an extra effort to keep in mind what she likes.

On an impulse, he reaches out and runs a finger over her lips. When she turns to face him, his eyes are steadily on her. She smiles, her eyes gleam with excitement while blushing furiously. 'You are so beautiful,' he says. She flinches and lowers her eyes. 'Would you mind to stay with me, tonight?' he asks.

'Why should I?' she softly responds, brushing her lips against his hand - even kissing it. There is nothing wrong with it it is not a disgrace.

'I have got something for you.'

'A surprise?'

'Not really. But yes.'

He scrambles to his feet and goes to his record player. Then inserts in a CD player and presses play on the remote controller. The song playing is an anonymous romantic soundtrack. 'What do you think about it?' he asks.

'Sounds great.'

'I wrote it for you.'

'What? You know how to sing?'

'Yes. Would you like to dance with me?'

What does she know about dancing? However, she allows him to take her by her hand and dances with him. She turns her gaze on him, and then a smile appears on her face. In her eyes, he starts to grow coquettish, frankly ravished. 'I like the beauty that you have.'

She lowers her eyes, smiling again. She is offering a blushing little smile as before. With a squirrel glance, he draws his lips closer to her mouth and kisses her.

Chapter Twenty-one

That is how they are supposed to live if she is pleased with him. On the previous night, she had a good dinner; slept well. In the morning, in his surprise, she wakes up early and slips out of the house. She enjoys his company more often, but she pretends to be hard to get used to. She spends three days without seeing him, locked in her room. She does not answer his telephone calls. Without warning her, he knocks at the door again at her apartment three days after the evening; she emerges from the bathroom, and opens the door, wearing a bathrobe as usual. 'You still angry?' he says when he sees her.

'Who gave you permission to come here?'

'I never thought I should be granted permission to come here to see my angel.'

Her face is pink he thinks he is becoming a bore; she has had enough of him coming to her apartment as it suits him. He does not notice that mood is feigned. She is silent, staring out of the window.

He takes her hand in his. 'Gladness,' he says, trying to keep his tone light. 'I'm worried; I missed you yesterday, and the other day. Are you all right?'

'Why wouldn't I?' she breaks off, gives him an impatient glare.

He pauses.

'Mind going out tonight?' he asks.

'You haven't answered my question.'

'Why are you avoiding me?'

'Everyone need some air.'

'So I bore you?'
'That's not what I'm saying.'
'What then?'
'Forget it.'
'Want to go out tonight?' he asks again but she does not reply. 'Please. I just want to introduce you to my parents.'
'Why?'
'Is it an issue if I want to introduce my lover to my parents?'
'No.'
'Then why should it be a problem for you to come?'
'I didn't say I won't. Anyway, fine I will come.'
Fine! Merely that way? Is she trying to get rid of him? These are her final words. If she says this, she will stick to it. He better learns it very fast. At a restaurant, he is sitting across the table with his mother; his father is sitting on the other side. She comes late, after twenty minutes. She is wearing a knee-length dress with a black smart-fancy-well sized coloured sweater and high heels, with a platinum necklace and matching platinum earrings. The family, the in-laws have not yet ordered anything for dinner. The mother's face is wearing a welcoming smile, so is the father when they notice her. Then she smiles back without meeting their eyes.
'Hey. I'm glad you came.' He pulls a chair and welcomes her to sit. 'Meet my mother, Teresa. And my father, James,' says Gill.
She first takes the father's hand; men always have to come first. Then takes the mother's hand. She pretends to be nervous to the extent that Teresa fails to take her eyes off her; she tries to keep her glance dropped with a little sheepish smile. 'You seem nervous,' says Teresa.
'I find it intimidating; I have never done this before.'
'Do you live around?' asks the father.

'Yes. St Patrick Street.'

'Is Francistown your home, were you born here?' the second
  question comes from Teresa.

'No, I'm from South Africa.'

'Really?' she is beginning to like her.

'Yes.'

'Tell us about your family.'

This is what she hates being asked. This question ruins
  everything. A pause, cautious. Then gathers herself, and
  swallows. 'My parents left me many years ago; I was only two
  months old. So, I grew up with my grandmother in South
  Africa.'

'Are your parents alive or…'

'They just disappeared. I do not know if they are dead or alive.
  My grandmother never mentioned anything deeper about
  them.'

'Have you tried to find them?'

'No.'

'Why?'

'I just don't feel like… I mean if they loved us, they would have
  come to visit us, and made sure we were fine. But they didn't,
  because they didn't care.'

'How many siblings do you have?'

'I just have a sister, she lives in South Africa.'

'How old?'

'She is my twin sister.'

'So why did you come here?'

She is not expecting so many questions. Especially about her life
  in South Africa. There is a long silence before she replies. 'Its
  business dealings,' finally she says.

She does not like talking about her family. Teresa likes her, she is a good child, she says to herself.

'I think I have to go now. Something just came up,' she pleads.

Teresa stares at her in puzzlement. 'Am I boring you, or I am just missing something?' she seems to say, but something cuts her words before she could open her mouth. Her words are subdued by parenthood when they come out.

'It's close to a midnight hour. You cannot walk alone,' says the father, glancing at her watch.

'I will take a taxi.'

'No taxis available at this time,' says the mother.

'I will take you to a hotel. If you want,' says Gill finally.

'Ohm…' she wears a doubtful look, but does not want to resist.

'Come let's go.'

She rises from the chair and picks up her purse on the table without meeting Teresa's defiant eyes. I have been there as well! Teresa thinks. She is suspecting something suspicious about Thandiwe. Then, she has no right to push her. Nevertheless, there is more time to spend together. She thinks she will take time to learn about her. When they get to his car, he holds open the passenger door for her. On the way to the hotel it is he and she, he tries to keep the conversation going. 'Why are you running away from my parents, are they scaring you?' Stupid question, your mother talks too much. I have been through it all; she can teach me nothing. I found you, so I cannot let her ruin my chance after all what I have lost. She seems to want to say. Even her voice, when it comes out, it is supposed to be serious so that he can clearly hear her. However, what she wants to say cannot be said. As a result, she softens her voice and pretends to be calm.

'I'm not,' she says.

'Because you said you wanted to go into your flat. However, I
am taking you to my hotel. Does it mean you have cancelled
your plan?'
She is silent, looking for something to say. Then, 'Since when are
you my advocate?' she asks. 'Are you making fun of me, or you
really want to know?'
'I was just asking.'
'I'm not your friend, Gill.'
'I was just saying.'
He pulls up at the parking zone of the hotel. He does not
mention anything on their way inside until they reach her
bedroom. 'This is where you are going to sleep,' he says. She
throws her purse on a sofa, eases off her shoes and lies supine on
the bed.
'What about you?'
'What about me?'
'Where are you going to sleep?'
'There!' he points at the bed on which she is lying. She rises and
takes off her sweater. She knows what is behind his decision.
She knows he wants to make love, perhaps the whole night. She
is right about it. She does not hesitate or pretend otherwise
because his desire is what she also wants. She draws herself
closer and kneels before him, touches his penis. 'You mind if I
touch you here?' she whispers.
'Nothing wrong with that.'
She loosens his jean inching it on the mat, on the floor. Follows
with his underwear, clears his body then crouches his penis. She
smiles; his breath becomes heavy. He stretches her out, kisses
her breasts; they make love. She is pleased with herself. She has
accomplished her plans.

CHAPTER TWENTY-TWO

The following morning, she wakes up at the hotel, a Maant-River hotel. When she wakes up, breakfast is set at the bedroom table. He has disappeared into the bathroom, she can tell from the sound of the bathroom water pattering against the shower room floor. An hour later, he returns, fully dressed, ready for work. She is pretending to be sleeping: the blanket is drawn to her chest, her eyes are closed, and her face looks the other side of the wall. When she opens her eyes, he is sitting on the bed; his hand runs through her cheek. He has been watching over her. There is a soft pop on her lips before she speaks. 'Hey,' she says softly.

'How was the sleep?' he asks.

She shrugs. 'Fine.'

'You look so amazing.'

Unusually, she smiles, showing a set of even white teeth.

'What are you doing this evening?' he asks afterwards.

'I don't know.'

'I will pick you up at seven at your flat then.'

'Where are we going this time?'

'It's a surprise.'

'Again?'

He runs his thumb through her face, then her lips. She closes her eyes, blushes. A long time since she last saw herself blushing so thoroughly. He draws his mouth closer and kisses her. 'I have to go to work. See you at seven; I will call to make sure you are ready.'

'Fine,' she says.

He disappears. Barely thirty minutes have passed since he slipped out of the hotel but he finds life very dull. He misses his own circle. He misses having the girl on his side. At the office, though he tries to give his work all his attention, the image of the girl does not escape him. The image of Thandiwe comes to him in a sudden and soundless eruption, as if he has fallen into a daydream. A stream of images of her smile, her voice, and her eyes pours down, images of the woman he has only known for two weeks ago.

The woman he has fallen in love with. Then the seven 'o clock evening hour arrives. He sends a driver to pick her up. When he arrives, she is standing on the sidewalks outside the apartment block. Unusually, she is in simple clothing: black jean outfits, with a white T-shirt and white ankle converse all-star sneakers. During the drive, he is taking her back to the hotel. The boyfriend is on the terrace, on the heliport. He has been waiting for her with a helicopter. 'Gladness,' he says when he sees her.

'Oh my God!'

He holds the door open as he ushers her in. The sound of it roars in the air, the engine of it sounds smooth enough. Sixty minutes on the airway, she spectates the city. She is viewing the city of Gaborone from its top. Weeks ago, she was a stranger to him, and today she has become an important person to him. She was a stranger, who once upon a time used to struggle with money, and now is living a life, better than the life she lived in South Africa. He is taking her on an outing, showing her life, showing her the other, unfamiliar world that she is greedy to

have. His company is enough to make her happy. This life does
not happen every day. It is not an everyday, every hour, every
minute living style, she tells herself. It is unusual in the quarters
of the country, the world itself. She counts herself lucky to have
escaped the incident of herself with August.

As days pass, she moves in to live with him. She counts herself
lucky not to be a lifeless woman this moment, running from
town to town, looking for a place to sleep, and asking for food.
The ritual with the healer has worked, regardless of the death of
him, she thinks. She ought not to mess up with her chance, her
good opportunity. When they return at his house, calamari
dinner is set on a table at the balcony. The balcony, a red cloth
on the table, and roses scattered all over the floor. The area is a
bit dark, offering a refreshing view of the city lights. 'You
hungry?' he asks.

'Yeah sure.' She glances around. 'It's so beautiful,' she says. He
draws a finger to her lips.

During the meal she tries to find a way of knowing him, asks
about him, about his living.

'What do you do for living? I mean how do you afford all these
expensive stuffs?'

'I have four companies. A construction company, and three
studios – two recording studios and a film studio. And I also
work as a commander in the military.'

'What about your parents?'

'My mother is an international medical doctor. My real father
was a solder, but he died in a war. So, my stepfather is a pilot,
he is never home most of the time.'

'When did your farther die?'

'I was seven. He was married to my mother, but she got married again when I was sixteen. That's the reason I usually regard James as my father.'

'Sorry about that.'

'Thank you.'

In the morning, before sunrise, she is awake on his side. Her body, completely bare. She wears his dressing gown, walks along the sitting room, past the hallway, and goes through into the kitchen. When he is wake, she is not on the bed. In the kitchen, he appears from behind. The smell is of fried foods. At first, she does not sense his presence; she is too absorbed to notice him. By the time she turns, he is upon her: he is kissing, stroking her.

'It smells so sweet,' he says.

'I wanted to make it a surprise, before you go to work.'

'I'm not going to work today. I have planned something.'

'What?'

'Let's go for cycling in the mountains.'

'You have a bike?'

'Of cause. Let's go for a shower first then breakfast later.'

The sun rose. A few minutes before eight 'o clock he brings two bicycles from the garage, one for her and one for himself. They ride into the mountains rocks. The shrubs are green, full of beautiful flowers. They slide aside, off their bikes and walk beside them through the flowers, approaching the river.

'Beautiful shrubs hey,' she says.

'How about we come up here for a picnic this weekend. What do you think?'

'Good idea.'

He glances over his watch; it has been four hours since they have
  been gone. 'Come let's go home. I hope the delivery is ready by
  now.'
'What delivery?'
'Don't worry about it. It's a surprise'
'What is it? I have reached the highest level of my surprises.'
'It's big. You are going to see it yourself.'
'Whatever,' she says climbing her bicycle.

CHAPTER TWENTY-THREE

On their way back home, they race towards the bridge through downtown gravel road. Through the ride, he is only listening to the crunch of the tyres on gravel pathway as she surges forward a curve and vanishes from his sight. In less than thirty minutes, she arrives at home. She leaves the bike on the pavement running into the kitchen looking for something to drink. Barely a minute later he arrives. 'You cheated,' he says.

'Let's just be honest, you are lazy.'

'You saw it yourself.'

He strokes her body, kisses her breasts on a point of making love. Gently, decisively, she wriggles lose. 'Not now,' she says. 'Where is the surprise?'

'Oh that? Follow me.'

With her eyes closed, he leads her outside, to the back of the house. Carefully, he leads her through the kitchen her by hand. Once they slip out of the house, he lets her open her eyes; they are on the family parking lot. She scans the lot and her eyes stop before a brand-new car. An Aston Martin vanquish zagato.

'It's for you,' he says. 'Do you want a test drive?'

'What?'

'What do you think?' he asks. From her, a glance cast with puzzlement.

'You bought me a car?'

'You like it?'

'Oh my God. It's so beautiful!' she jumps on him screaming in
her joy.

'Do you like it?'

'I love it!' She nips the back of his neck, and runs her tongue in
his mouth. Then she slides into the car. He lets her take the
wheel, while he sits, occupying the passenger seat. She reverses
into the street pavement, and then takes the township road.

She feels nothing inside her about him but she gets all attention
she needs from him. In return, she has to make him see her in a
good way, with a different eye. He is everything that she needs
to revive the state of her finances. The following day she fills
her room with pictures for memories in her affair with him. She
plays the role of a wife. In the evening, she cooks a five-star-
worthy meal of his favourite dinner. Before he comes, she
switches off all the lights in the bedsit room and makes a path of
candles that hints to the table set in the middle of the room.
When he arrives, he is tired. She takes away his briefcase and
invites him to seat. Then brings some oil and offers him a back
massage to help him lessen fatigue from a stressful day. Perhaps
she is not able to give him the best massage he has ever had, but
he somewhat seems to enjoy that she is trying to assist him.
Months pass, he packs his suitcases and leaves for Australia on a
work trip.

During the days of the trip, he cannot figure himself out. He is
too restless to sleep at night. Each morning he heads for the
mountainside and sets on a long jog. As of today, he is a happy
man, with a beautiful girl that he wishes marry. Time lies before
him to spend as he wishes with her, with the perfect woman he
has been blessed with. The feeling of loving her is unsettling; he
doubts it will ever settle. For each day, he tries finding time to
stay in contact with her. In the evenings he telephones, stays on

the line as long as he wishes. Then the mornings after, he spends it on Skype. Then, she is not a creature to miss people. There are days that she wishes to spend without him, without seeing his face, without the sound of his voice. She is tired of his presence, tired of men who behave like children. She stays away from the telephone, from the cellular, often stays away from her computer MacBook. He has been taking all his efforts to make a sort of daily or weekly ritual to give her a sense that the two are closer, despite the distance. He is becoming a bore sometimes, so she has begun to avoid him. This is just the beginning of it.

CHAPTER TWENTY-FOUR

Though he is aware of himself being a bore to her, he has no wish to let her go. He is tired of living on his own; he would like to have a soft hand. He needs a soft hand to comfort him, assist him start a family. He does not know how to handle her; she is a total stranger whom she has never dealt with. Saturday afternoon, he returns to the country. When he arrives, she is nowhere to be seen. She returns on Monday evening. Though it irritates him, he does not have a wish to say anything to her. His usual response is to withdraw into silence. He tells himself that he must be patient; women have different temperaments when they are on their mensuration cycle, a burden of every woman. Maybe he is wrong. Maybe he is the problem. There is only one explanation to her irritating mood: she does not take pleasure in anyone.

On Saturday, he takes her to a museum. After that, a paintball. When they return, it is dark. He takes her to the bedroom, clears her body, undresses himself and slides under the sheets with her. They make love she does not withdraw. Without the two of them making love, she will also become a bore to him. She has a duty to share herself. On the bed, she does not own herself. She lets him be the one who leads; she is the one who follows.He plans another trip, a trip with her to the other side of the word. I just want to make things look right for her, he would be saying. He books a modern expensive guesthouse in Le Mas de la Tannerie, Gordes, Vietnam. A honey-coloured stone walled impressive guesthouse. All rooms are coloured with a monochrome -and some have private balconies, from which there are views of the surrounding olive grove and distant Alpines peaks.

All have soft linens and cashmere blankets, hand-painted tables and re-upholstered flea market finds. In the smart bathrooms, there are stand-alone tubs and polished-concrete sinks. They check in on Thursday in the evening. When they arrive, at the open door is a Vietnamese young woman older than Thandiwe. She is wearing a welcoming smile, 'this must be Mr. Martins and Miss. Gladness,' she says, taking their bags into the bedroom. 'Come, I will show you around.'

She strolls showing them the bedrooms, the kitchen, the living room and the entertainment area.

'What do you think?' he asks Thandiwe.

'I think it's best. What do you think?'

'Nice.'

'Where is the terrace?' she asks the hostess,

'Outside near the swimming pool, mam.'

'Can you show us around?'

'I will lead the way, mam.'

As for Gill, he is in the grip of something, but he waits until supper. After the meal, he orders a basket of sweet treats for dessert, and hides the gift amongst the chocolates. In a chocolate sauce around the rim of a dessert plate, there is a message for Thandiwe.

'Gladness. This chocolate cake is not big enough to show you how much I truly love you. You are the best I have ever had in my life. Will you marry me?'

As soon as she lifts up the chocolate, a ring box falls on the dessert plate. He allows a pause to develop, which in return he wants Thandiwe to fill with her comment. It seems she does not

have a word for it; perhaps, she does not want to be married.
She accepts the proposal.

CHAPTER TWENTY-FIVE

They return to the country on Sunday evening. She seems not happy that she will soon be married. Something deep inside her is not right; she remembers growing up not wanting a husband in her life. Now, today, right now, the husband has come, he is in her life. She has to make a way of dealing with it. When he is at work, she slips the ring from her finger. She does not even want to see the design of it. When he returns, she slips it back. Though he has taken her to Vietnam and asked her to be his wife, as long as she does not want to be married, his company remains a problem to her. The problem that is growing, slowly becoming a big matter that she will not be able to handle. She disappears for days, for weeks. Although he is becomes his own investigative sergeant to track her down, his mission does not succeed. At night he becomes a ghost, the situation does not die. He is not improving, he stays up all night, waiting for her but she does not return. He does not even have appetite.

She returns on Monday after three weeks, in the morning before the sun rises. When she opens the door, he is waiting for her in the living room. She does not notice him: It is still dark and the lights are off. 'Gladness!' he says, turning on the lights. 'It's three o' clock in the morning. Where have you been?'

She does not look up. 'I was out getting some fresh air.'

'You have left for four weeks now, and you say you were getting fresh air?'

'Look! I'm tired now,' she says. 'Can we talk about this later? I need to rest a little bit.' She does not wait for his response; she takes the stairs and vanishes from the scene.

'Gladness come back her. I'm talking to you!' he shouts, but she evades him in return. Then sleeps in the spare bedroom.

For a few minutes as he is sitting in the living room, the telephone rings. It is work — over the phone, his general wants him to be at the solders' camp before six o'clock in the morning, the same day. There is a war in Afghanistan, and he must be on it, says the general. When he puts the telephone down, he goes straight to the shower, packs his stuff and leaves. He leaves a letter on a table in the bedroom, where he sleeps with Thandiwe. Two days after that he has left, she wakes up at eleven am when there is someone knocking at the door. She rushes downstairs and immediately opens. The face that she sees in front of her is of a total stranger. A face of an old man, who is wearing a soldiers' uniform. He is striding through the front door, impatiently sniffing the air.

'Miss Gladness?' asks the old man.

'Yes. What can I do for you?'

'I have bad news for you concerning your husband, Mr. Martins. He was called by General Raphael to be at the camp on Monday morning, to get ready for the war in Afghanistan. The war was very violent, I am sorry to have this sad news for you but Gill Martins is no more. He is no longer with us. He could not even make it on his way to the hospital in the ambulance.'

Her eyes turn reddish as tears discharge. Back in her heart, she feels a surge of hurt. He says nothing more. He knows it will hurt her more than she seems. He also feels sorry for her. 'I'm very sorry,' he repeats and closes the door. Then leaves, she is left alone in the house. She regrets her waywardness towards him.

CHAPTER TWENTY-SIX

Two days after the incident, she reaches out to the letter he had left in their bedroom. It reads:

'Dear Gladness. I write this letter to apologize for not being a good husband to you. I know I should not have pushed you, put you through the pressure that I had in me. I am sorry I lost faith in you, and I want you to know the following. Before I met you, I used to wonder if there was a purpose in my life. However, when I first saw you, I believed the universe was giving me a chance to see the purpose that I have for the life that I live – that I love you. You had your reasons, and I understand all that. I still love you more for that. With all the love in the world, I want you to be aware of your importance in my life. These final days with you have been the finest of my life. I hope to see you again when I come from the war, but if I do not, remember that I always love you. You are the best deepest love of my life, Gladness. I will be watching you from the stars.'

'Forever I will love you. Gill.'

Now that the boyfriend is no more, a dejection overtakes her. Standing against the wall in the living room, hiding her face in her hands, her chest heaves and heaves and she finally cries. She ought to remember: no matter how heavily she will cry, Gill will not return into her life, she will never set her eyes on him again.

She will see his flash only once in the coffin, on the day of his burial. Then from that day, she will only see him in the photographs. Seven months ago, Teresa has been in Morocco, working on her new surgery. Now when she returns home because her son is dead. She has been on Thandiwe's case, investigating her. When she returns, she has all her information: her names, her address in South Africa. She also has information about Catherine. The day that she returns is a day of tribute for her son. She waits for a few days before she glosses over it. After the burial, the same Saturday, she finds Thandiwe sitting on the sofa, wrapped in a black shawl. She puts a hand on her shoulder, 'follow me,' she says and disappears into the bedroom. Barely a minute later Thandiwe has followed as ordered. There is deafening silence before Teresa speaks. She is wiping off the tears on her cheeks.

'Whatever that has been happening between you and my son, it is no excuse that he is no more. But I wanted it to stop,' she says.

Thandiwe is silent.

'I know you,' she repeats. 'I know who you are. I know about Catherine, about your sister. I know about your father, Themba.'

Now it is her chance to speak. She stands tongue-tied; the oxygen does not pass through her lungs. Teresa is right; she has a grandmother and a sibling, too. How can she deny it?

'How do you know about my father?' she asks after the silence.

'I was married to Themba. We lived in the same house with Catherine, but we had to move. But a few years after we left, Themba died.'

She is silent again.

'I know Catherine did not tell you why we left.'

She watches her closely, but gives no sign of comprehending. Her senses tell her that Gill was her brother. It would only make Teresa her mother. She is wrong Teresa denies it. The truth is refusing to come out; she refuses to tell her about it.

'Don't let it be a problem. It will be better to hear the truth from Catherine herself.'

'No, this is madness...'

'It is not your fault you fell in love with your brother. But it is better to hear it from Catherine, as I said,' says Teresa and returns into the living room. It is either Thandiwe has not understood, or she does not believe it.

Chapter Twenty-seven

The days of herself living in the house of the dead boyfriend are numbered. Her life is like that one of a little bird in a nest, waiting for its dead mother to come back to feed it. She has given him pleasure, the one that she had a duty to share with him on the days of his life. She has been having thoughts of returning to South Africa, but she is still living in the shadow of grief. She waits for a few weeks before she makes her mind, waits for things to fall into place. Nothing goes accordingly; her nights remain spooky to her.

Then one Friday evening she packs her bags. She clears the wardrobe and clears her makeup drawer. In the study room on the desk are her two framed photographs with him, she takes them with her too. Minutes before noon on Saturday, she is driving on Harrismith road, passing Cayingubo train station. At lunch hour, she has reached her destination; she pulls up behind the closed garage door. From the garden Thandeka comes. For a moment, she does not recognize Thandiwe. Six year have passed, and she has put on weight, her skin has turned lighter. As soon as she notices her, she bursts into tears, wipes her hands, and holds her arms wide, embracing her, kissing her on the cheek.

'I'm sorry,' says Thandiwe as she tries to fight off tears.

Though she has returned, the memory hangs uneasily over them. As for Thandeka, she is only happy for having her; she is back into her life as a sibling after all. She has come home, returned alive and safe. In the living room, she sets her juice and biscuits.

Catherine appears from behind; at first, she thinks Thandiwe is just a stranger. She is halfway in the path towards the kitchen before she recognizes her. She soon catches up with them; by the time Thandiwe turns, the warmth of Catherine's chest is on her, warmly embracing her. 'Thandiwe?' she cries.

'Grandma,' she reaches out.

The evening falls, they eat in the kitchen at the table: sesame noodles with chicken, but Thandiwe is in no mood for it, she has no appetite. She dawdles her chopsticks through the noodles. The need to know, to find out the story of the parents does not escape her. At once, in a point of crying she starts talking. She talks, telling them about everything, touching all of the incidents. She glosses over her affair with Gill, mentions the words of Teresa, even mentions the marriage proposal, and the death of the boyfriend. When she is done, she gives Catherine the chance to speak. She lets her who should speak, speak. She has to tell the story, tell all of it, and let the children know where they come from. The moment of it has arrived without a warning, it is like a fish caught by an eagle when it was diving at the surface of the warm sea. She has a chance to wriggle out, deny it. Then, how can she deny it? The story of it is like a joke. She has long ceased to be surprised at the range of arrogance of Thandiwe, the child that grew up in her hands. She lowers her eyes, very ravished. Thandiwe is asking sensitive questions, the secret begins to frighten her. 'Shall we not talk about this now? It has been a lonely place without you,' she says.

'I have nothing else to talk about except this. I need answers!' she says grimly.

She would like to refuse with it, but the truth cannot be barred, not anymore. It consumes her night and day. Yet despite everything, regardless of all the good and bad moments, the truth is supposed to be told. No matter what happens now, they will have to live together as siblings, as grandchildren and a grandmother. However, the words are not simple as a child's livelihood. She ought to formulate them before she says them.

'What do you want to know?' she asks.

'Everything!'

This is her own confession. She gives an impatient little flick of the hand. 'Don't blame yourselves, my children. You would not be expected to do anything. And I'm sorry I kept it in me for a long time, but the truth is that I'm your mother,' she says at a point of crying.

'What do you mean?' asks Thandeka.

She is silent, trying to find a perfect way to explain it. She still has a chance to lie, but she has no future with it. 'I'm your mother... I gave birth to you,' she is pointing out at them, 'both of you.'

'What are you saying?' says Thandiwe.

'Themba is my son, he was my only child. He was a husband to Teresa, too. But I was having an affair with him.'

'Your son is our father? And you are a mother to us?' asks Thandiwe.

Cathrine nods mutely.

'You slept with your own son?' asks Thandeka.

'Yes.'

They are all silent.

'It's nice for you to say it. A shameless old woman on top of her own son! *Pwyeuuuu! Sies man!*' Says Thandeka and rises from her chair. She meets Catherine's eyes defiantly and disappears from the scene.

'Thandeka, please! At least try not to make the situation more complicated than it already is,' says Thandiwe.

She disappears all of the night hours, and she is nowhere to be seen. She returns to the house three days later at midnight. The atmosphere here is still not good for her, she would like to disappear, leave for good. She goes to bed and wakes up before sunrise the next morning. She has no appetite; she turns off the lights in the living room, and then slips out of the house. Treading cautiously in the dark, she approaches her car, but shunts into Catherine in the garage door.

'Thandeka, I know I have done something disgraceful. It is bad enough it happened. But you can't keep avoiding me this way!'

She does not bother to reply. Her face is strained, puffy with anger. She avoids her, tries to leave.

'I'm sorry…' Catherine repeats. 'You're sorry but it means nothing! Nothing at all!' Thandeka shouts at a point of striking her.

'I know…'

'So?'

She takes time to respond, trying to find something in her mind.

'Goodbye! I'm late for work,' she repeats.

'I know being sorry explains nothing. However, you are fortunate I am alive, Thandeka. You heard the truth from me. In addition, probably there is daylight left in me. You still have a chance with me, as your mother. Do not play with it because you never know, it might be your last time talking to me right here. So it's your choice.'

Whether she understands or not, she begs no pardon. On the contrary, she slings her bag over her shoulder.

'Goodbye, Catherine!' she turns and dodges from the scene. In the garage, she opens the garage door, slumps into the seat of her car, and reverses into the pavement and drives away.

An hour later, she parks the car at the hospital's parking lot. It is still dark, hours before the sunrises. She tries to go back to sleep in the car, but cannot fall asleep. She slips out of the car, wears a jacket over her shoulders, and goes into her office. The same noon becomes a mess, a tragedy. A destruction, and distress, it is like a serious accident, crime, or natural catastrophe. Catherine tries to give them time. She knows when to leave the two alone until the event dies down a little. She toys with an idea to step back from them, let them dwell on the situation. Giving them time alone allows Thandiwe to think over the situation. She must not be too mad about it. She is always silent because she has nothing to say. She also has destroyed peoples' lives.

She is in a state of profound wellbeing she understands the situations. Nevertheless, getting to accept it must be so hard for her. She has seen the commitment Catherine has had to her, to Thandeka too: she has given up everything to prove how really she fell in love with them, to sacrifice, risk anything for them, not as a grandmother, but as a mother. Then, for Catherine, it sometimes gives her no reason for herself to live in disgrace. I should have told them the truth long time ago, she would be saying to herself, but it is too late for her to return to the old days. Unless there is something that can be added to her life.

She makes a decision, but no one has to know anything about it. Perhaps she is being very rash, but she should proceed with her plan. She makes up a bed for herself in the spare room. At night as the midnight hour approaches, Thandiwe and Thandeka are fast asleep; she is awake lying with a sheet drawn up to her face. She pushes aside the sheets and opens the wardrobe. For a few minutes, she casts a look inside it, glancing at David's, her dead husband's neck ties slanged all over his suits. She picks the tie he wore on the day of their wedding. At six thirty in the morning, as the first birds are beginning to chirp, Thandeka is awake. She goes into the kitchen wearing a bridesmaid dressing gown her face is very haggard. She prepares a pot of spicy eggs and potatoes for breakfast. When she looks out through the window, vaguely, she notices a human body in the trees near the garden. She comes out of the house in total bafflement to see Catherine's dangling body hanging on a branch of a tree.

She chokes in a sudden surge of pain, which she cannot take anymore. She screams and faints. Thandiwe could not hear the sound of her voice, but in a sudden rush, she is on the scene. 'Thandeka!' she calls out falling on her knees, and trying to wake her softly and urgently. She is terrified by the body of Catherine on the tree, but keeps her eyes on Thandeka, fearing to look at the body.

CHAPTER TWENTY-EIGHT

Now that Catherine is no more, Thandeka is suffering from insomnia. It will take her a long unpredictable time. Even after the burial, the feeling remains unsettling. As from today she knows who is to blame, it is no one but herself. She often toyed with the idea of going to work more often, presuming she would get used to it. On Saturday, the hospital is not busy, but she is at the office trying to work as usual. In the same afternoon, she hears a knock on the door. She cannot believe another miracle. August has returned, without invitation, he enters consciously, and waits in front of the desk. He has been gone for longer than she can remember. 'August?' she says. 'What do you want?'

He is silent, looking for something to say.

'Look, you might be very handsome and all that, but it does not mean I am dump...'

He cuts her off. 'You are angry, I understand. You know I try but I am not good at apologies. I just need one more shot at a second chance because... I'm missing you!' He says.

'Too late.'

'Like I said I'm ready to make any sacrifice, not just to get you back. I am going to keep my promise, never treat you like a follower again. I swear!'

Her words are so serious that he can see her anger. 'That is what you said when we first met! Listen, today makes it almost six years and six months since you have left me all by myself. Don't

you somehow think it is time that we make it clear? I tried
August, but I'm tired.'

'I know I have let you down. But I'm sorry.'

'Save it! You have ten seconds before you are out of that door
before I call security.'

He tries to convince her, but his request is too much for her.
Though he is aware that she still takes pleasure in him, he
believes he ought to keep a distance from her. He ought to give
her time to let things settle. He is sick of the sound of his own
voice and sorry for it indeed. He withdraws while she trails on
his behind leading him straight out of her office. She ought not
to trust his hype. The same afternoon it goes bad at work – the
whole week gets worse. Though she has got rid of him, he still
finds a way to come to her. He comes up through her mind, and
lingers. Her mind has become a repository for old memories of
herself with him. She ought to chase them out, sweep her senses
clean. However, she does not have anywhere else to put them.
The more she tries to sweep him out, the more he comes to her
mind. In addition, the death of Catherine remains a problem
too.

Presently, she comes out of the hospital at ten in the evening.
When she gets home, she tosses in bed withoutnany sleep.
Finally, in the middle of the night, she falls asleep. A vision of
him comes to her: he is striding through the bedroom door,
waiting patiently, watching over her. He wishes her no harm;
he is merely warding off the bad spirits. Perhaps it is a good
vision for her. Her alarm clock rings for her to get ready for
work on Wednesday morning.

CHAPTER TWENTY-NINE

As for August, he does not prefer to keep himself at a pitch of anger, though depression still falls on him. The feeling of it is merely neutral. He is able to sleep well sometimes, but he regrets having an affair with Thandiwe. He tells himself that he ought to be patient with Thandeka, and then things will fall into place again. He does not bother to find out how she feels about the story of himself; he already has an idea of how it feels. Two weeks after he has come from Britain, the Busamed hillcrest hospital telephones him. They would like to work with him as usual. The work must start on the Monday of the following week, says the manager. On Saturday, he takes with him a fiber spin mop, angle broom with dust Pan, a bottle of aeroshine and a doorway tiara into his office, the office that almost look like an old home since he left it. He still has the key of it, but when he arrives, the door of is open. Thandeka is inside, but the office is thoroughly a mess: a mat of dust and sand has caked on the floor. Pieces of paper lie scattered all over the floor. Plastic takeout containers and wine corks are tumbled out into a wicker Basket. Food in the refrigerator has expired. Gingerly, Thandeka lifts the mess of it into a plastic packet and ties it tightly.

'I imagined you might need a hand,' she says as soon as she sees him.

'How did you find out I was coming?' he asks.

'No need to hesitate.'

Tiptoeing around the office, he finds a photograph of himself with her on the day of their marriage. He passes it to her. 'Do you remember this?' he asks.

'At our wedding,' she remarks.

Once the work has been done, he takes her out for lunch. Then afterwards, he takes her back to their house, in Pietermaritzburg. Things have begun to fall in place as he thought. He ought not to mess up again, otherwise he will regret it all of his miserable life. In the middle of the night, he is at ease as she sleeps beside him. Hours before sunrise he opens his eyes and turns on the light; Thandeka is leaning on his chest, with her eyes open too. 'Good morning,' she says drawing a sheet around them.

'Hey. What time is it?' he asks.

'Four o' clock in the morning.'

'Why are you up so early?'

'I have been watching over you.'

He is silent before he speaks. 'I sincerely apologize for the grief I have caused you. I ask for your pardon.'

'Listen, I want you to do one thing for me.'

'What is it?' he asks.

'I want you to forgive yourself. You are a good man, August. Believe it.'

In the morning, they set cornflakes and tea for breakfast. The chance that he is given is for himself to be happy, and let everyone have a chance to be happy for a day too. Two weeks pass, Thandiwe decides to return to the university and finishes her course.

CHAPTER THIRTY

Despite all, Thandiwe still finds him entirely adorable. Nothing has changed; she still has the same feeling about him. By seven, with dawn touching the hills and the dogs beginning to stir, she is awake. She has not forgotten how it felt in the cold winter mornings in the uplands of the KwaZulu Natal in his arms. She wants to make her life with him – wants to get along with him. How can it be possible when he does not belong to her? He is her sister's husband. Let her not forget it, she ought to respect it. Hands in pockets, she is in the garden, wanders around the flowerbeds. A cold mist hangs over the plants; her nose even drips when she tries to work out the tomatoes. A memory comes to her; she remembers when August had to be her sweater in these cold days. Out of sight on the garden, her cheeks are wet with tears. She comprehends how she misses Catherine even though she has brought the bad part of herself to her; she has carried the secret for almost the whole of her life. For a few days she tries to let the situation settle in her, let it die, let it all go to hell, she thinks. On the contrary, it becomes worse; she toys with an idea of seeing August. A week after her decision, before sunrise, still an hour or two away, she is awake. It has been one of her sleepless nights.

Before nine in the morning, she is outside, at Thandeka's house, waiting at the frontal door. Her car parks at the sidewalks outside. There is a smell of beacon, which reminds her of him. One of the Sundays, he had served her breakfast of bacon and eggs when Thandeka and Catherine had gone to church.

Sometimes when she misses him, she forgets how she has hurt Thandeka. From behind the closed door, she hears voices, a voice of a man and a woman. They are talking, and laughing. Once things fall into place, she knows it intimately: it must be Thandeka and August. For the fact that she still wants to be with August, it irritates her when she sees him with Thandeka. She is vexed, angry.

No longer is there friendliness in her physiognomy. She drives back to Ladysmith, returns indoors, and packs her rifle and the cartridge of it. I must get rid of one of them, she says to herself.

When she returns to Thandeka, she uses a different route. She must cover her own tracks, she thinks. She ought to close the chapter, forget that she once slept with him, but she plays the sniping agent. She tip toes through the shrubs but blunders through the flowers in the mountain before she reaches Thandeka's house.

I am going to be kicking up a fuss, she thinks. Her whole body radiates violence. She approaches the house from behind, and waits from a distance, then starts with the mission. She loads the cartridge with the calibers, and runs her eye on the eyepiece. She holds her eye to it, in order to capture a good sight. She is aiming at her targets. Through the eyepiece, she notices them; they are sitting at the table, on the patio. They are eating breakfast. August is speaking, she has no idea what he is saying, but every now and then, there is a nod of agreement from Thandeka. He rises from the chair and kisses her.

She is still working on the parallax, adjusting it. Once she has found a proper sight picture, her graticule is completely visible and solid. In the center of her sight picture, she has aligned with her target. The graticule is on Thandeka's parietal bone. She drags her index finger to the agenda. However, before she squeezes, tugging it, she first thinks of Thandeka, thinks about the grief she has caused her.

She changes her idea and shifts the graticule to August. Aiming at him, she thinks about her own family. He and Thandeka are the only family she is left with. She pleads with herself. She wants to make up for the wrongs of the past, but this is not the way to do it, she says to herself. If she fails to stand up for herself at this moment, she might never be able to hold her head up again. She might as well die, and leave nothing. She retires from the mission this cannot be done. Not now, not again in her life.

She returns indoors and cracks on a giggle of tears. This is her life this is where it begins. From today on, she is on her own. She is the one who has to live here. What happens to her is her own business, hers alone, not August's or Thandeka's. Where she is now is where temptations have led her. She is a daughter of her brother, though it is not her fault. Then, she has fallen in love with her niece-brother, and she is carrying his child. She will be a mother soon. She must prepare for it. Thandeka and her husband will no longer provide for her. That has all gone, gone with the wind. She will have to learn from her own sister to work hard, and get married too. No emotion: no need to cry, her own life has been lived recklessly.